Canyon of Death

Scott L. Miller

Parker Publishers ,7345 W Sand Lake RD, STE 210 Office 3266 Orlando, FL 32819.

Requests for permission or other information should be addressed to Parker Publishers ,7345 W Sand Lake RD, STE 210 Office 3266 Orlando, FL 32819.

This is a work of fiction. The events described here are based upon historical events; the story and characters are fictitious and not intended to represent actual persons or events.

Ebook: 978-1-967840-09-0

Paperback: 978-1-967840-10-6

Hardback: 978-1-967840-11-3

Published 1993

Printed in the United States of America

First Edition

I would like to take this opportunity to acknowledge the editorial comments and suggestions of two of my closest friends, Jean Hawley and Cynthia Wevers, whose thoughtful contributions greatly enhanced this work.

This book is dedicated to all the Viet Nam Veterans. The dead who will never return, and the living who are still trying.

Prologue

1867 somewhere in the present-day Southwest

The Apache scout allowed only his eyes to move as he watched the canyon below. He had remained perfectly motionless below the ridge line that was just now being tinged by the sun as it crept over the mountains to the east. As the darkness began to recede in the canyon below, he spotted some mourning doves gliding like gray ghosts into a small pocket of water hidden within the rocks. He also was able to pick up the sounds of the approaching wagons. It was the same group that they had attacked earlier. After a long last look, he silently withdrew.

****

The heavily loaded wagons crept slowly up the steep shelf of rock – rock which had provided a suitably wide trail since it had begun on the canyon floor. The wooden spokes of the wagon wheels creaked in protest as the steel bands of the wheel rims cut through the pine needle carpet. The rich wet soil beneath the wheels clung like glue. The morning sun sent long fingers of pink and gold through the flanking peaks while the floor of the valley was still shrouded in predawn darkness. Even at this early hour, the heat was starting to build. The leader reined in his horse, a powerful sorrel, and looked backwards at the line of men, animals, and equipment. The effects of three months on the trail since leaving Mexico City were evident. Man and animal alike, looked exhausted and spent, no longer resembling the best of the French army. He had to laugh despite himself. It was a bitter and sardonic sound. He was a highly trained officer. His men were experienced troops, the best France had to offer, and where were they now? Some God forsaken mountain range in the middle of an Indian country.

The trip had been extremely grueling. The country had taken its toll of men, animals, and equipment. The surrounding harsh countryside, a constant reminder of the contrast to the remembered lushness of France. But more than this was the Apache. None of them had ever encountered fighting men like this. European battlefields were a glorious blend of pomp and tradition where flags flew while orderly rows of soldiers advanced towards one another through shot and shell. Here it was hit and run tactics. The enemy would not stand and fight, and this system of combat had thoroughly demoralized his troops. The skirmish of three days earlier had cost him another three men and most of the remaining provisions.

He had awakened in the early pre-dawn darkness and realized that he had a new set of priorities. First, he must rid himself of the freight wagons, and then he had to get his men to a safe place. They had to have an opportunity to rest and recover their strength if there was to be any chance of completing the mission.

The mission had been entrusted to him by Maximilian. Maximilian, the answer to all the trouble that occurred in Mexico. The trouble being that a group of liberals, led by Juarez, confiscated much of the property from the local populace. These people had promptly gone into exile in France, where they convinced Napoleon the Third that Mexico could be regenerated with a Catholic prince and the French army. Thus, Maximilian had been appointed Emperor upon accepting the Imperial Throne of Mexico on April 9, 1864. Thinking of Maximilian, he pondered, as he had done so many times before, on the twists of fate. Here was a man close to his age, a man whom he had envied many times in the past. He had envied the position, power, wealth, and women. And now Maximilian lived in fear of losing his very life at the hands of that renegade Juarez. That fear was the very reason for this expedition. He recalled very clearly the night he had been summoned to the palace in Mexico City and been given his orders by Maximilian himself. He was to take command of a large shipment of gold disguised as a freight train. Gold that Maximilian had spent the last two years hoarding. This accumulation of wealth was the result of carefully holding out, a little bit at a time, the wealth that was to be transported to France and Napoleon's coffers. The shortages had not been suspected, or if they had, were certainly not being investigated.

He was told that once out of the city, he was to follow a north-northwest direction until he intercepted the wagon road leading to San Diego. There, he was to place the gold on the first ship bound for Europe. The entire mission was to be conducted under the tightest security. Maximilian was beginning to suspect that the French troops guarding the imperial Throne were about to be withdrawn. He knew that if they were withdrawn he would not stand a chance if he remained in Mexico. Thus, the gold was his only hedge if he did have to make a run for it.

The sound of distant hoof beats announced the return of the advance scout. The officer raised his right arm and brought the column following behind to a halt before riding ahead to receive the scout's report.

Reigning his lathered mount to a stop, the scout said, "I think I've located a suitable place, sir."

The officer motioned for him to continue.

"About two miles ahead the trail flattens out onto a small mesa top. The mesa abuts a sheer rock face on its far side. At the base of the rock face is a natural tunnel of about fifty feet before opening into a large cavern. The cavern is large enough to hide the wagons with room to spare."

The two of them sat on their saddles in the morning sunlight while considering this information. The only noise that broke the silence was the sound of the scout's horse as it noisily sucked in great lungs full of air, its gray sides heaving.

Chapter One

1941, Gila Wilderness, Southwestern New Mexico

The faint trail continued upwards through the country and progressively got rougher. The early afternoon sky was starting to fill with thunderstorms coming in from the west. He was well above the meadow where the rest of his herd grazed. He couldn't figure out what had caused the calf to head up into the mountains. There wasn't any sign of a predator or anything else that caused the calf to leave the safety of the herd. A remembered axiom laid down by his father caused him to smile. "Stock don't have to have a discernible reason, from the wandering calf to the well-broken mount who kicks when touched in the same spot that has evoked no response the previous six hundred times. They do what they do when they do it. Rhyme or reason be damned."

The young rancher continued to sweep the ground in front of him. The brim of his Stetson pulled low on his high forehead, shielding his sea-green eyes from the sun. He still sat comfortably in the saddle though he had been at it since sunup. If he didn't find the calf, before long he would have to give up and return to camp. Shadows played fitfully across the trail as the encroaching storm clouds played a game of hide and seek with the sun.

Canyon of Death

The trip was already a day longer than planned, and if he wasn't home soon, Meg would have a search party out looking for him. He hated the thought of losing the calf. Running a single-hand outfit was an "iffy" business at best and the loss of the calf would be a financial hardship. But he couldn't let his neighbors mount a search for him when there was no need. Riding on accompanied by the scent of pine and the creaking sounds made by saddle leather, his thoughts turned inward.

After all, he had been very lucky with his stock. Since his father's death three years earlier, this would only be the third loss. The grazing permits his father had been able to obtain after the re-designation of some of the Gila Wilderness acreage to primitive status in the early thirties had passed to him upon his father's death, and for that he was grateful. This was a good grassland. But he was most grateful for his new bride, Meg, now some three months pregnant.

The trail finally crested on a broad mesa top, butted by a sheer cliff on its far side. The only cover was at the very base of the cliff consisting of several large boulders and a stand of young Douglas fir. Focusing an intent gaze on that general area, he saw a flicker of movement. The calf changed position and then seemed to disappear in front of his eyes. Riding closer, he noticed a natural tunnel opening which had been hidden behind some trees and boulders. He tied his horse to a young sapling and, after removing his rope, he entered the tunnel.

Standing just inside the entrance he let his eyes adjust to the interior gloom. After a few minutes, he could see the calf backed up against the rear of the tunnel. He approached slowly, swinging his rope with practiced ease. He let the loop float down over the calf's head. As he was leaving, he noticed with little interest that what he had taken for the end of the tunnel was loose rubble from a cave-in.

He was on his way home by late afternoon.

Chapter Two

John 1964

Los Angeles

It was one of the very few summer days when the sky was a brilliant blue and the few clouds were snowy white. As John strolled out on the sun-kissed tamarack of the Long Beach airport, heading towards the TV station's hanger, he could already feel the heat starting to build. He enjoyed the job. The "job" consisted of flying the traffic copter while his cameraman filmed the snaking freeways below, and he provided comment.

Just as he finished sliding the hanger's corrugated doors open, he heard a voice from behind.

"Hi John, great day to fly," said Roger, his cameraman.

"Yeah, it is."

They had been a team for two years. They usually got along quite well despite having two completely different personality types. John could be described as adventurous, devil may care, whereas Roger was down to earth, by the book, let's not ruffle any feathers.

They lifted off to start the daily patrol. They usually picked up the 405 and headed north with Redondo Beach, Hermosa Beach, and Manhattan Beach to the west, skirting the airspace around LAX onto

Marina Del Ray before turning east at Santa Monica until Interstate 5 where they turned south until reaching Orange County Airport turning north back to Long Beach. They flew the same basically circular route 7 days a week. At first, it had been fun but now it was becoming mundane. John felt a sense of disquiet, a need to look for something different. After all, there was nothing holding him here. No romantic entanglements. He could find a job anywhere. He had been thinking of joining the military. The way he saw it Viet Nam was starting to heat up. There was probably plenty of excitement for a chopper pilot. He decided to talk to a recruiter when they finished today.

His thoughts were interrupted by a high-speed pursuit unfolding below them. Two highway patrol cars were pursuing a beige-colored sedan southbound on the 405. As he turned south to follow he noted that the early morning traffic was still sparse when measured against the overwhelming freeway commuters in about an hour. Momentarily, out of the officer's sight, the sedan took an immediate right-hand exit onto 73 towards Laguna Beach. The pursuing CHP did not see the exiting sedan and continued southward on the 405.

John dropped down towards them. "What are you doing?" Glancing over he could see that all color had drained from Roger's face. "They're going to get away and I think I can stop them."

The sedan had stopped at the end of a closed street. Several things happened at the same time. Roger placed the chopper between the sedan and the only exit, CHP arrived, and the two suspects were taken into custody without incident.

They took off and continued their normal flight path. When they landed, they learned, after being swarmed by reporters, that the suspects were fleeing a double murder.

Trying to avoid any notoriety John pushed through the crowd and entered the hangar where the station manager told him he was fired for his actions and the FAA representative told him his license was suspended pending a review.

******

Later that night he was sitting at a bar in one of the many Gentlemen's clubs adjacent to LAX. A stranger approached, "Are you John Perry?"

Thinking he was another reporter, "No comment."

Sliding onto a vacant stool, "1 can offer you two things. One a job and two your license returned with no restrictions."

"OK, explain."

Twenty minutes later, they shook hands confirming his acceptance of working for Air America which the CIA used as a cover operation for clandestine operations in Laos, Cambodia, Thailand, and Vietnam.

Chapter Three

1967 - North Vietnam

The mission had gone very well and Zack had reached his extraction coordinates just before dawn. Concealing himself in the thick growth near the edge of the natural clearing, he settled down to await 'dust off'. His inner thoughts focused on the phrase, 'dust off.' The more he thought of it, the stranger it sounded, as words will if repeated over and over. Finally concluding that it was a strange phrase for a helicopter extraction, he let his mind go blank. The jungle had returned to its normal rhythms of sound and movement within minutes, following the slight disturbance caused by his arrival.

The eastern sky was growing lighter and the temperature seemed to be matching it, a degree increase for every ten minutes. It was like sitting in a sauna full of rotting vegetation. He didn't move as sweat formed at his hairline, broke through the band encircling his forehead and coursed down his face. Within moments, it was running freely down his sides, back and chest, pooling in his groin. As the day advanced, he became a sopping wet mass. It seemed every insect in Southeast Asia was crawling in and out of every orifice of his body. Still, he did not move.

The sun had climbed higher and Zack estimated that it was around ten o'clock when he heard the first sounds of movement through the jungle on the far side of the clearing. He wasn't surprised. He had been there too long. Something had happened to his ride out of there. The jungle growth was too dense to determine their exact position or number, but that didn't make much difference. They had to be North Vietnamese regulars and that meant that he was in a lot of trouble. Continuing to remain motionless to avoid detection and capture, he asked himself two questions, what in the hell was he doing here in the first place, and where was his ride? For an operation that went so well, this one was sure getting fucked in a hurry. The only thing that had seemed odd was the speed with which he had returned to work. Normally, he was given ten days rest before he was returned to the field. Not this time.

Returning to base from another sector the day before yesterday, he had been subjected to a mercifully short debriefing and was on his way back to his hotel room in town. He was anxious to get back to his room. It was the one oasis in an otherwise insane existence. One of the perks of this job was the reluctance of the local brass to allow his group to reside on base. Hell, maybe they were afraid of contamination of the mental kind. If so, then one had to wonder who they were afraid would contaminate whom. After all, they were all there for one thing - to kill. The only difference was that the majority were there to kill without discrimination, he and his group were there to kill specifically.

Unlocking the door to his room, he walked in and hit the light switch on his way to the refrigerator which was humming quietly in the corner. With an ice-cold beer in his hand, he paused to turn on the stereo before shedding his jungle fatigues and entering the bathroom to draw a very hot tub.

After the water cooled to an uncomfortable degree, he stood and dried off. Using his towel to wipe the steam from the mirror, he stood studying his bearded face. It was a strong face, dark complexion with a single scar across the bridge of a prominent nose. His sea green eyes returned the steady gaze. The mirror, having been hung for a man shorter than his six-foot frame, he stooped a bit to comb his jet-black hair which hung below his collar line. He once again concluded that his reflection, though not handsome, was at least not ugly. In the past, it had been called competent. He liked that.

His quiet contemplation was interrupted by a knock on the door of his room. Throwing a towel around his waist, he moved to open it. Pausing before drawing the inside bolt, he pulled his forty-five from under his discarded clothing, and holding it behind his back, he opened the door. It was John. John was as close a friend as he would ever find or allow himself to find in this place. In this type of environment, you did not allow anyone to get too close. They had a way of turning up dead. He didn't say a word as John passed by him and handed him the twice-sealed envelope.

Tearing open the envelope, he read the short message from intelligence. Great, they had messed up another one. They had given him the wrong target and now he had to go back up there and do it again. Taking a wooden kitchen match from the box on the end table, he walked back into the bathroom and burned the message. Watching the ashes disappear down the flushed toilet, he couldn't help but wonder how long he had before **he** disappeared. He had been operating in this area for almost a year. One year and eight targets. He had begun to believe that he was living on borrowed time. Walking back into the living room, he felt John's steady blue-eyed gaze focused on him.

"What's up?"

He paused before answering. He knew that John didn't expect a detailed answer. Zack couldn't give him one anyway. However, as a friend, he was looking for some information.

"I've got to go back up-country. Seems as if the intelligence types fingered the wrong man and now it has to be done again."

"I kind of figured something like that. I'm supposed to hang around and give you a lift out to the air base. You're due to take off three hours from now," John said while stretching out on the couch

Zack was briefly irritated by the offhand carelessness of the response until he remembered that John couldn't possibly appreciate the strain he was under. John never had to be in the bush. As a chopper pilot, his job was to fly into and out of it, not occupy it.

Still, the offhanded remark stung.

Zack turned towards the bedroom. "Look, why don't you pour yourself a beer or something while I get ready?"

John went over to the built-in refrigerator and pulled out an ice-cold San Miguel. Pouring the amber fluid into a chilled glass, he called out to Zack.

"You know that you have no one to blame except yourself. You could have stayed a regular Marine officer but that wasn't exciting enough for you. You had to go and get yourself recruited by the CIA and become an assassin."

Listening from the bedroom, Zack caught the odd tone of his friend's voice. Contempt? Confusion? Concern? He wasn't sure.

Catching the look on Zack's face, he walked into the living room with his gear. John adopted an air of mock exaggeration and said,

"Oh, excuse me. I forgot that the preferred words are 'The Company' and 'Spook' not CIA and assassin."

This time there was no doubt, the concern showed clearly in John's voice and face.

The ride to the airport was uneventful and some two hours after takeoff, he stepped through the door of the solid black unmarked DC-3 used for clandestine operations. There was that delicious sensation of total weightlessness, free of falling sensation, despite hurtling through the night sky at 120 m.p.h. The opening shock as the black canopy of his parachute snapped open indicated that all was well. He felt the jungle below long before seeing it. Even at this early morning hour, it felt warm and humid. He landed without incident, buried his 'chute' in a shallow grave, got his bearings and proceeded towards his objective.

After an hour on the trail, the outbuildings became visible within a clearing about twenty yards ahead. He crept closer until he could make out the whole compound. It was what he expected to find. It was the former home of a French plantation owner. The ranking officer's retinue of personal guards was on constant perimeter patrol. A ground force penetration attempt would have been suicidal. But then again, he didn't plan on a ground force attack. His night glasses brought the target into view on the second floor of the villa, third window from the left. The French doors leading from the bedroom onto the balcony were left open to catch even the slightest breeze. Zack raised his night scope and the room jumped into focus. He saw the VC colonel and what he initially took to be a woman. They were stretched out on a large canopied bed. The mosquito netting was rolled up on all four sides and tied securely under the eaves of the canopy, supported by the ceiling-high bedposts at all four corners. When she turned toward the window, Zack saw that he had been mistaken, she wasn't a woman at all. She was a young girl of no more than fifteen or sixteen. She had the look of a typical peasant girl, shoulder-length thick black hair, cut in bangs across her forehead. Soft brown eyes sat on either side of a pug nose set above a full mouth. Continuing to see through his night scope, Zack noticed the vacant look in those eyes as the colonel absentmindedly stroked her naked thigh. Placing the cross hairs of the sniper rifle's scope on the man's left temple, he took a deep breath. As he slowly exhaled, he allowed the pressure of his trigger finger to steadily increase. The bullet took the man cleanly through the left temple, expanding within the brain cavity and exiting through the right side of his head above the ear, leaving a hole big enough to stick your fist into.

The girl started to scream hysterically as blood, bits of bone and brain tissue exploded against the wall above the headboard and sprayed across her chest and face.

Zack already began his withdrawal by the time the guards started to react to the noise and confusion coming from the upstairs bedroom. Merging into the darkness, the jungle embraced him like a long-lost lover; wet, humid and pulsing with the promise of life and death.

****

They were closer now. With a sinking feeling, he realized that they would have him unless a miracle occurred. They continued their sweep of the undergrowth and had almost passed him by when one of them stopped directly in front of Zack and opened his trousers to take a leak. Looking down, he saw Zack crouched in hiding. They had him.

Chapter Four

1972 Chicago

It lay there mocking him in its pristine whiteness. He knew what it was, had known since entering the empty house hours ago. He knew what it was, no need to open it. He knew it as surely as he knew that when he finally went upstairs that all of Julie's clothes and cosmetics would be missing from the master bedroom and bath. Things hadn't been right between them since he had come back. Oh, she had tried, she really had. The doctors assured them both that he would recover from his wounds, both physical and psychological. She had been so patient and then he was finally given a clean bill of health and things still didn't change. The physical 'clean bill of health' was a lot easier to achieve because it was measurable. The bone was knitted together or not, the wound healed or not.

On the other hand, the psychological, Zack was soon to discover, could take forever. He paid attention when he talked to the base shrink, and the more attention he paid, the more it dawned upon him that 'they' didn't want Zack and the others helped as much as 'they' wanted a demonstrated success rate. As surely as an x-ray demonstrated a healed bone, a series of well-paced affirmative statements demonstrated a healed mind. And a healed mind was the ticket out. The ones who weren't able or couldn't see the logic in this approach were labeled as being in denial and were quietly dealt with.

He was dead inside, couldn't connect with any other human being. Incapable of maintaining or establishing any sort of intimacy. Yeah, he was dead inside and nobody knew it but him. Because everyone either ignored his time in Nam or reviled him for it, none would ever find out. He would never trust another person enough again to talk about it. That was just the way things were, so get on with life. Just get on with it.

Ignoring the marble-handled letter opener, he tore the end of the envelope with an impatient yank and slid the single sheet out.

He was right, she was gone.

He threw the paper down onto the desk and picked up the only piece of mail delivered that morning. Doing so, he felt an odd anticipatory combination of excitement and fear. The feeling was an exact duplicate of the feeling he got in Nam just before combat. Adrenaline rushed through his veins with such a positive force, he felt as if he could ride it, much like an untamed horse. The difference between bravery and cowardice in life, he mused, was whether one faced one's fear or hid from it. The postage indicated the letter had been following him for some time. The embossed return address on the upper left-hand corner of the rich cream-colored envelope bore the name of Rutherford Attorneys-at-Law. Upon opening the envelope, (this time he used the letter opener), Zack found a letter from old man Rutherford himself. Lord, he must be close to ninety by now. The letter explained that the enclosed envelope was a letter to be delivered to Zack on his thirtieth birthday. Rutherford went on to explain that this was the only request of his father before leaving town in July of 1942 for basic training. His firm had honored the request and as such was finished with the matter. There was a brief paragraph at the end, 'hope you are well, etc.'

Zack felt a little strange after opening the enclosed letter. He had never known his father or mother. His mother died giving birth to him and his father was killed in the South Pacific in 1945.

Zack was only three at the time of his father's death and was being raised by his aunt and uncle who owned a ranch just west of his father's place. He continued to live with them through high school and then moved to Albuquerque to attend UNM where he graduated in 1965. Then he married Julie, joined the Marine Corps and left for Viet Nam almost immediately. Zack realized that he had been holding his breath. Letting it out with a sigh, he settled into one of the dining room chairs and tore off the end of the enclosed envelope. The letter began:

July 15, 1942

Dear Zackary,

The fact that you are reading this means I am dead and that we never had a chance to meet and get to know each other. For that, I am sorry, but circumstances beyond my control have dictated this outcome. There are many things I want to say to you but time is short and I feel compelled to tell you of one event to the exclusion of all others. I want to tell you what happened to me in the fall of 1941.

I had been out trailing a missing calf for two days. When I saddled up on the morning of the second day, I was thinking that if I didn't find the critter pretty soon, I would have to give up the trail and return home. We couldn't really afford to lose the animal, but I also couldn't afford to be away from your mother and the ranch much longer. By mid-morning, I was ready to give up when the trail started to slowly flatten out and dissolve into a broad mesa top which was flanked at the far edge by a sheer rock face. The only cover was at the base, choked by some Douglas Fir and boulders. I didn't see the calf until I got pretty close; he had found a small tunnel to hide in.

Anyway, after getting him out, I started home. I was about halfway down the mountain when it occurred to me that what I had originally mistaken as natural rubble at the back of the tunnel was actually rubble from a blast. I couldn't figure out why anyone would blast a tunnel that far back in the mountains. Then I remembered the stories I had heard as a young

24

boy tending cattle. The story of the French soldiers and Maximilian's gold. Until then, I had thought they were merely stories to entertain a kid, but now I think there may be something to it. I don't know why, I just do.

Son, I know that life has started pretty rough for you with the loss of your mother and me. I don't know if the man is still there for you or not. I know that your uncle has done the best he could to raise you right. I want this to be given to you on your thirtieth birthday. I chose that date with the hope that you will have achieved the maturity to take the responsibility for your decision. I have no doubt that you will try and solve this mystery. The decision I refer to is what to do with the gold when you find it. You will find it, I have no doubt.

All my love,

Dad.

Zack stood there holding the letter as emotions washed over him. Sadness over the lost parents that he never knew, remorse over his recently failed marriage, and an almost indescribable feeling of freedom and sense of purpose that he hadn't felt since leaving Viet Nam three years ago. He also realized that he was his father's son. He would go after the gold; it was the only legacy his father left him.

Chapter Five

It hadn't taken him long to close out his affairs in Chicago. There weren't any friends and he had a walkaway job. He had decided to take his time and indulge in a long-held fantasy. During his childhood, Route 66 had represented a road to freedom and adventure. It had even been immortalized in John Steinbeck's novel The Grapes of Wrath and in more recent times by Martin Millner in the TV series 'Route 66.'

So, on the 10th of July, he loaded his suitcase into the battered VW Bug and headed south out of Chicago on a clear bright summer's morning. He picked up old Route 66 at St. Louis and followed it through Joplin, Tulsa, Oklahoma City, El Reno, Amarillo, Tucumcari, and Santa Fe. Heading south out of Santa Fe on the 15th of July, he reflected that the date may be prophetic – the same date as his father's letter, albeit thirty years later. The morning sun was just cresting the Sangre De Cristo mountains as he cleared the outskirts of the city and gained access to Interstate 25, the only north/south artery in New Mexico. He watched as the early morning's light played on the east-facing slopes of the many and varied mesas off to the west. The sight took him back to his early childhood, and the joy he had felt watching the intricate patterns of

Canyon of Death

light and shadow as they played across the eroded sandstone. He had forgotten how beautiful the landscape of his home state was. By the time he had passed through Albuquerque, the sun was at its zenith, leaving the Monzano mountains in a shimmering haze of heat. He followed the lush green of the well-irrigated land stretching southward in front of him, lending a sense of false coolness when compared to the sunbaked land to the west, until he arrived on the outskirts of his old hometown by late afternoon. Not much different except a new Dairy Queen that was built next door to the Greyhound bus depot and across the street from the Grange Hall. The more noticeable change was in the air of decay permeating the town like the rank smell of a dead skunk in July. The store fronts with their dirty and cracked windows, the dusty sidewalks, the empty streets all reflected the malaise associated with general economic collapse. Zack had been reading about the large conglomerates buying up the local farms and ranches for large-scale operations, leaving the former owners with little choice except to move on. He had not, however, been prepared for this. He had been out to his uncle's place earlier in the afternoon. Actually, it was his uncle's former place, having been purchased after his death by one of the larger conglomerates. They hadn't done anything with the land or buildings and the whole place was slowly going to ruin. The ridge pole on the roof of the main

27

house broke and the roof was sagging badly. All the windows were broken out and the front door, supported by only the top hinge, leaned drunkenly against the jamb. The outbuildings didn't fare any better. The barn was allowed to collapse and now lay in the dust with its broken timbers sticking up out of its grey and weathered corpse surrounded by a host of tumbleweed pallbearers. As he walked around, Zack saw that the family hadn't had much luck with the land; first his father's ranch lost to taxes, followed by the loss of his uncle's place to developers. Following the visit to his uncle's place, he accomplished three tasks. He checked into the local Motel 6, telling the clerk that he was a freelance journalist researching a story on the demise of the individual rancher in favor of major conglomerate control. Pulling out of the motel's parking lot, he headed back north toward the town's only used car lot. On the way in, he noticed a 1969 International Harvester Scout that he wanted to take a closer look at. The VW took good care of him in the city and on the trip down. But now that he was heading into some very rough country, he wanted the ruggedness that only a Scout could offer. Ten minutes later, he turned left off the main thoroughfare and passed under a garish sign saying 'Sam's Used Cars' in neon script that was dark in the afternoon heat. A large sign to the left of the front door of the small square office building stated that Sam's carried their contracts, had no credit check, and would take payday payments. Zack smiled to himself. From the prices whitewashed on the windshields, he had no doubt 'Sam' could afford the risk associated with clientele who couldn't afford a conventional loan. The lot was arranged to attract the majority of high credit risk clients. The young with all the high-priced flashy sport models along the street side; middle-priced family models towards the center; and trucks and industrial types along the back fence. The salesmen gathered at the front of the office came to life. He pulled to a stop and just as quickly dropped back into their lethargic state when Zack waved at them and turned towards the back fence. He had been looking the Scout over for several minutes before he was approached by one of the salesmen. "Looking to buy yourself a four-by-four, are you?"

"Not at this price."

"Why, that there is about as fair a price as you could find. These Scouts are a good vehicle. They stand up to hard use real well. Yes, sir, $8,000 is a fair price."

"I'll give you my VW and $2,500 cash."

"I'll have to talk it over with the lot manager."

"OK."

The salesman walked to the office and disappeared inside, reappearing with a middle-aged man dressed in slacks, loafers, a sleeved white shirt, and a red necktie loosened sufficiently to allow room for his considerable Adam's apple. They were talking in a low voice, which stopped as they neared Zack.

"Understand you want to buy that Scout."

"Yes. I told your salesman here that I would give him the VW and $2,500 for it."

"Can't do it for less than the Bug and $4,000."

"I'll go to $3,000 and the Bug."

Twenty minutes later, Zack pulled back onto the main thoroughfare and headed south towards town.

His next stop was the local sporting goods store where he proceeded to outfit himself with a high-quality backpack, lightweight tent, sleeping bag, camp stove, cooking gear, and a large supply of dehydrated food. As he approached the counter with his supplies, he saw her for the first time. She was helping a customer select a sleeping bag. Zack watched her, and was immediately drawn by her sense of self-assuredness. As he drew nearer, she turned toward him. He noticed her startlingly clear grey eyes for the first time.

"Can I help you?" she asked as he laid his selections on the counter.

"Yes, you can ring this up and I also need some of that insect repellant, the Evergreen brand."

As she started to total his purchases, he continued to study her. She was pleasant enough to look at, though at 5 feet 3 inches, a bit shorter than usually attracted him. But there was something else. Just as she started to become aware of his intense gaze, he broke the silence.

"You're Pam, aren't you? Freddie Coleman's little sister?"

She looked at him very closely and started to smile.

"Zack, Zack Johnson. Is that really you? I don't believe it. It's been what... Eleven or twelve years, hasn't it?"

"Yeah, I guess so. I left for UNM in 1961 and I haven't been back since. How is Freddie?"

Pam's smile faded.

"He was killed during the TET offensive."

"I'm sorry to hear that. I didn't even know that he was in the service, let alone in the country."

Pam seemed to shake off the memory of her brother's death and her smile slowly returned.

"What are you doing here anyway?" she asked.

Zack paused before answering. Did he want to tell her the same cover story he had given the motel clerk or did he want to tell her the truth? He had known her almost all her life, but then again, he left town when she was a kid of fourteen. And eleven years was a long time. Things and people change. He decided to play it close for a while.

"I'm a freelance writer and I'm down here on a combination research/vacation trip. If you would like, I can tell you more over dinner tonight."

Pam fixed him with a thoughtful gaze while she pulled absentmindedly at her shoulder length strawberry blond hair.

"I get off at five. You could pick me up then."

With a nod of acknowledgment, Zack picked up his bags of purchases and turned toward the front door.

On the drive back to his motel room he was thinking of how much Pam had changed. From a tomboy with dirty hands and knees to a fully mature female with the most hauntingly beautiful eyes he had ever seen.

****

He was up just before dawn the next morning after loading his gear into the scout. He drove out of the motel parking lot at daybreak. Driving north from town, he glanced to his right and saw the early morning sun beginning to send salmon pink rays through the Caballo mountains. The wind blowing through the open windows of the Scout was cool and still damp from last night's unexpected rain. The water-soaked scent of sagebrush and mesquite was delicious and triggered an image from last night's storm. They decided to drive into Las Cruces for dinner. Sitting facing west, they were enjoying both their drinks and the sunset when the first loud clap of thunder startled them. Looking through the north-facing windows towards the sound, he was amazed at the sudden buildup of clouds. It was a solid black mass stretching from horizon to horizon. Lightning flashed almost continuously, lashing out from the inky blackness of the thunderheads' base and licking the mesa tops with blinding flashes. Within minutes, the rain hit. The downpour was fierce, lasting for perhaps fifteen minutes before the storm swept on southward. The storm had been both too brief and too violent to do much good. A long, soft, and gentle rain was what was really needed to refresh the parched landscape and bring new life to it. Funny, he thought, how quickly the land returns to you. In Chicago, he couldn't ever remember assessing the rainfall. This morning it had been an automatic reflex.

He swung west on State Route 152 at Cabal. Passing through Hillsboro and Kingston, the old mining towns brought back memories from his childhood. He always enjoyed his uncle's stories about the gold and silver that was discovered there. He remembered the first strike was in the late 1870s and resulted in the formation of Hillsboro, with Kingston being founded some ten miles to the west in 1880. He had especially enjoyed the stories of the Apache and their frequent raids on the settlers. This constant harassment caused the U.S. Army to build four forts within a forty-five-mile radius. By 1882, the eastern slope of the Black range became somewhat safer as a result of General McKenzie's efforts in the area.

At San Lorenzo, he turned north on State Route 35 to County Road 163 and then continued north-northwest.

He found the dirt track he was looking for and swung north-northeast. The track was faint at best and several times he thought he had lost it. He was glad he bought the Scout 4x4 when he arrived in town. When he saw it on the wholesaler's lot, he remembered being attracted to them as a kid on his uncle's ranch. His uncle swore by them. They weren't deemed pretty by most people, rather square and boxy. And they were neither fast nor easy on gas. What was it that he had heard? Something like, "My Scout gets 20 m.p.g., 10 cities and 10 highways." What endeared them to their owners was their virtual indestructibility. They were equipped with either 304 or 345 cubic inch V8 and could move incredible loads over some of the most unforgiving terrain imaginable. He eased down into and out of yet another wash and was once again thankful for the high-centered transportation he chose.

The sun climbed high overhead in a sky of cobalt blue. A few puffs of snowy white cloud hang over the western horizon, giving an illusion of the potential for more rain later in the day. Spotting a reasonably flat surface ahead, he decided to stop for lunch. He packed all his gear in anticipation of today's noon meal. Pulling out the ice chest, he placed it on the lowered tailgate of the Scout. He placed his backpacking stove next to it and assembled it. He was using a model known as a SCORPION. It consisted of a round bowl shape about the size of a silver dollar containing four collapsible legs. When these legs were folded out, they formed the cooking platform. In the center, an element with a neoprene fuel line attached to a small butane cylinder was placed. When the butane was turned on, this element could be ignited. Placing his tea kettle on the stove to boil water for instant coffee, he got out his bread, sandwich meat, and mustard. In a matter of minutes, he was hunkered down, on the shady side of his truck in the soft sand, with a mug of coffee and his sandwich.

Eating his sandwich, he noticed a hawk off to the west riding the thermals. The sight made him feel good. He always considered the hawk his good luck sign. He marveled at the graceful ease of the bird as it allowed the updrafts of heated air to carry it with seemingly little effort on its part while it searched for its noonday meal. Slowly, the hawk swung away towards the Mogollon mountain range.

Finishing his lunch, he picked up the area and then proceeded north-northeast. In late afternoon, he crested a low rise and caught sight of his father's former grazing lands. The dry wash he selected for that evening's camp provided cover for both the camp and his vehicle. While preparing dinner, he reflected on how old habits never die. Although he was on public land, he automatically chose the least obtrusive spot for his camp. It wasn't that he feared the results of accidental discovery, he just wanted to avoid it. His evening meal was a quick and easy mixture of beans and rice with bread, washed down with several cups of coffee. Finishing his meal, he did the few dishes and then rolled out his sleeping bag. Laying under a velvet black sky studded with stars, he let his mind wander. It quickly settled into the familiar theme of the past few weeks. Was there any gold? Would he find it?

Chapter Six

The Chevy Caprice was southbound on Interstate 25. There was not much to distinguish it from the other early morning travelers. The grey paint was scratched in several places and the body had a few dents. Even the coat wire antenna, though a bit unusual, didn't look really odd or anything. The headlights picked up the eastbound turnoff for U.S. 70 and after making the turn another ten miles, brought the car up to the main gate at White Sands Missile Range, WSMR to the locals. At precisely 0430, it was waved through the gate and turned toward the main building complex snuggled up against the eastern slopes of the Organ mountain range.

The parking lot was deserted. The sole occupants were the light standards bearing their fluorescent burdens high above the jet-black asphalt with its orderly spaced white lines.

The grey Caprice proceeded toward a reserved space in front of base security. Coming to a full stop, the lights were extinguished and its lone occupant got out, slammed the door, and went through the main door.

The hallways of Base Security were quiet and sparsely lit as Chief Master Sergeant Chuck Harkness made his way to his office. Entering, he turned on his desk lamp to diffuse the predawn grey.

The early morning sun had been highlighting the peaks to the east when he pulled into the parking lot, but it was still a good hour until full daylight. Easing his 5'9", 200-pound frame into his swivel chair, he ran his hand over his head, disturbing the few remaining red hairs. He had to think, get a grip on himself. He wanted to be together – had to be together when he saw the old man. He hadn't come this close to retirement to be cheated out of it now. It had been too damn long in coming.

It seemed impossible that the time had gone by so quickly. Had it been almost thirty years since he had stood in front of that dried up old man sitting so prim and proper in his black robes all set to pass sentence on him while he stood as a sniveling seventeen-year-old thief? He could still visualize that stern face peering down from the impossibly high bench and in a thin whisper of a voice giving him a choice of jail or the service. The offer was not that unusual at the time; World War II had just started and the peacetime army was desperate to swell its thin ranks to a wartime complement.

He chose the army, but unlike other men given the chance to straighten out their lives, he had chosen to continue his criminal ways. Europe was ripe for a man of his talents and when the war ended, he decided to reenlist. By that time, he was a staff sergeant and a staff sergeant's pay wasn't too bad. He had been able to miss action in Korea and thought he had it made until Viet Nam started to flare up. He had to laugh when he remembered how mad he had been when his orders for Da Nang Republic of Viet Nam had come through. Had he gotten out at 20 years, he would have missed the whole thing, but after looking at the difference in retirement pay when you compare 20 years to 30 years, he decided to stay in the service and thus, was eligible for a Nam assignment.

Viet Nam turned out to be a bonanza of opportunity for someone like himself. If a person wanted to make a lot of money, the varieties of ways available were almost limitless. As a senior NCO in the military police, he was in an enviable position. The black market had been very lucrative and it hadn't taken long for him to get into prostitution and drugs. After volunteering for a second tour, he had concentrated on drugs to the exclusion of all else. Shortly afterwards, he met Colonel Dotsero, although at that time, he wasn't a colonel. He had been a captain acting as a liaison officer between the CIA and the military. It was to prove to be a marriage made in heaven or hell, depending on your viewpoint.

Harkness had made some good contacts in the Golden Triangle, that magical area where Thailand, Burma, and Laos connect and the opium was plentiful, rich, and sweet. He established a sound, consistent supply of very high-grade opium and was making a very decent profit.

Dotsero had been using a few of the local drug lords as informants. They were very useful in pinpointing the location of top North Vietnamese officers and officials. This information was indispensable in setting up assassinations and kidnap operations. In return for their help, the CIA used their private air force to move drugs for the locals. This air force didn't exist officially, nonetheless, Air America was alive and well.

He would never forget the first time that he had seen Dotsero. It had been quite by accident. He and a local big-time drug dealer named Lang had been doing business for about three months. Lang was well connected with the local officials and was able to operate without much of a hassle as long as he kept a low profile. Harkness was just entering Lang's camp on the Thai border. The camp was in a small clearing and consisted of two main buildings. One was Lang's hut and the other larger one was a barracks for his men. The only other structure in the compound was the cooking hut. Jungle growth pressed in tightly around the perimeter bamboo fence enclosing the encampment on three sides. The south side was open and that was where the corral for the pack mules was located.

Running parallel with the corral's back fence, a slit trench reeking with the smell of human excrement baked in the sun.

The monsoon season was in full swing and the air was thick with humidity. It was like breathing through a thick hot wet towel. A storm was marching in from the west and the late afternoon sun was reflecting off the base of the monstrous thunderheads towering up to some 30,000 feet causing crimson streaks to appear in the otherwise jet-black mass. Lightning occasionally flashed, licking the jungle below with a forked tongue of heat. Although the approaching storm was still several miles away, the air was charged with energy, making the storm a palatable force.

Dotsero and Lang were just exiting Lang's hut when Harkness stepped out of the jungle into the camp's clearing. Before he could step back, Dotsero spotted him. Harkness had no choice except to continue across the compound toward them.

Dotsero was the first to speak, "Who are you?"

"I was about to ask you the same thing."

Dotsero took a deep breath and fixed Harkness with a hard gaze. Before he could say anything, Lang stepped in between the two men.

"May I suggest that we return to my hut and continue this discussion in private?"

Both men nodded in agreement and followed Lang to his hut. They entered the typical one-room structure made of bamboo and palm fronds, and settled around the only table in the room. Lang took a bottle of Johnny Walker Red from a shelf near his elbow and poured a drink for all of them. Then draining his glass in a single swallow, he said, "Gentlemen, it seems as if my business matters have overlapped to a degree. This is regrettable but I suppose it was unavoidable in the long run. I am now going outside and leave you both to work out any difficulties that you may have between you."

Dotsero settled back in his chair and studied Harkness. He only needed a few minutes to formulate an opinion he could trust. In his line of work, you formed the right opinion quickly or you were dead quickly. His impression was that he was facing a career noncom trying to feather his retirement nest. Probably some black market, drugs and prostitution. Harkness was also sizing up Dotsero. Although he knew of Dotsero (in fact, knew a lot about him from the information he gathered over the last few months), he had never seen him in person. In truth, he had been avoiding any contact. It wasn't that he was overly concerned. He just couldn't see confusing his life by letting Dotsero become aware of his presence, at least not until he found some way of using him.

Dotsero spoke first, "You're a long way from home, aren't you?"

Harkness started to speak and was cut off as Dotsero continued.

"Look, I don't really care who you are or what you're doing. I just want you to understand one thing. If you cross me or get in my way, they'll never find your body. Understand?"

Harkness sat in disbelief. What was with this guy? Why was he coming on so strongly? Was he afraid someone was going to cut in on his turf, or did he have something to hide? He decided to lay his cards on the table.

"I don't know why you're so tense. There's more than enough action for both of us. You see, I know who you are and what you're doing. I know about the labs and I know who else is involved. Hell, a man can't spend this long in a country without figuring out what's going on and, if he's a mind to, cutting himself in on the action. Also, before you get any cute ideas, you should know that all this information is back in the States. You know the routine. I disappear and it gets published. Trite, but true. So, instead of getting uptight, maybe we can just live and let live."

Dotsero had sat perfectly still through the speech. In fact, he hadn't so much as twitched while Harkness was talking. Only two things were moving in the room; a gecko lizard stalking a fly on the wall and the beads of sweat rolling down Dotsero's face, dripping onto the backs of his hands which lay passively in his lap. Harkness was beginning to wonder if he was human. Dotsero finally shifted his weight and said. "OK, so assuming you know about me, why don't you explain who you are and why we should 'live and let live'."

"Look, I've established a network of distributors throughout Thailand, Laos, and South Viet Nam. I know the CIA is moving drugs in exchange for information on enemy locations. I also know that it wouldn't take much for you to cut yourself in on some of the refined product. So, I was thinking, what if we combined efforts? You get the use of my network for additional contacts and I could pick up some extra cash by cutting out the suppliers."

Harkness was looking into the faded blue of Dotsero's eyes, watching for a reaction. Seeing none, he continued, "Of course, there would be some financial remuneration for you. Basically, that's the plan. If you're interested, we can work out the details later."

Harkness had thought he had an opening when he was asked to explain his plan. He knew he had found a kindred spirit when he finally saw the flicker of interest in Dotsero's eyes. Dotsero confirmed his observation a few minutes later.

They worked well from the beginning. The war continued to drag on and their Swiss bank accounts were starting to reach a comfortable amount. That was when they had made their first mistake. It sounded so reasonable, almost foolproof when the opportunity presented itself. A chance to move a massive load of heroin. They had reached the point where one big sale was all they needed and they would be set for life. Yeah, the first mistake had been greed all right. Even though they had all their bases covered, even though they had planned it to the Nth degree, they hadn't paid enough attention to Zachary Johnson, and that had been their downfall.

Who would ever have suspected that a spook would have a conscience? Zackary did. Unlike others of his ilk, he had a strong sense of morality and while he could kill an enemy without any emotional involvement at all. He became very emotional about drugs. It hadn't always been that way, but the death of his high school sweetheart from an overdose changed him forever. He was well paid to kill the first category. He would always take care of the second group free of charge whenever he had the opportunity.

The success of Dotsero and Harkness was due in large part to not drawing attention to their operations. They had been successful for so long that they became complacent and that complacency led to their downfall. They had forgotten that it was the little things that could foul you up.

The little thing that had started the whole disintegration was Zackary's discovery of the drug operation. It had happened quite by accident as these things usually do. Zackary had just returned from a mission and was on his way to his quarters when he had spotted Dotsero's jeep parked in a side street in front of an abandoned warehouse. Without thinking of the whys and wherefores, he had decided to investigate. The front door was unlocked and he was able to ease into the building without being seen. As his eyes adjusted to the interior gloom, he was able to make out an office built on a platform that ran the whole width of the building half-way up the back wall and tucked in below the beams supporting the structure's massive roof. It was then that he was first aware of the tables and glassware that were the components of a drug lab. Just then the lab lights came on.

Zack watched in disbelief as Dotsero held out a briefcase to another man whose face was hidden in the shadows. As the man stepped forward to receive the case, the light fell across his face and Zack recognized Lang. He had heard rumors about Lang for some time and now they were confirmed. Lang opened the briefcase revealing a large amount of cash.

"It's all there," said Dotsero.

"Then your shipment is assured. Delivery will be made on the tenth of next month in the usual way. If there is any change, I'll get word to you or Sergeant Harkness."

Dotsero left first. Zack waited in the shadows until Lang extinguished the light and started toward the door. As Lang moved past him, Zack dropped the loop of his piano wire garrote over his head and simultaneously pulled on the small wooden handles set in the wire's end while placing his knee in Lang's back. Lang's body went rigid for a brief second and then limp as his nearly decapitated head fell back, still connected to his body by a few shreds of flesh. A huge gout of blood sprayed over the door, Zack and the briefcase.

Zack picked up the briefcase and hurriedly left, making only one stop on his way back to his quarters and that was to throw the briefcase over the wall of the Catholic orphanage.

Zack confronted Dotsero with it the next morning. Storming into Dotsero's command post, catching him alone placing colored pins in a large wall map. Dotsero turned at the sound of the slamming door. "What the hell do you want?"

"I want to know exactly what you and Harkness think you're doing!"

"I don't know what you mean, and I'll thank you to keep a civil tongue in your mouth, Lieutenant!"

"Fuck off. I know all about your little drug scam. Did you two really think you could keep it quiet? Did you really think you would get away with it?"

The accusations hung in the stillness of the room. They stood there glaring at each other until the sound of the air conditioner's compressor interrupted the silence. Dotsero spoke first. His voice was as cold and calm as the surface of a Montana duck pond in January. "Get out."

Zack stood for a minute or two in incredulous silence, then left the room displaying the same icy calm as Dotsero. Dotsero picked up the phone immediately and called Harkness.

"We've got a problem."

"What is it?"

"Zackary Johnson. He knows about Lang, you and me."

"Has he told anyone yet?"

"I don't think so. Look, I want you to contact Lang. We've got to figure this out before Johnson is due back."

"Back?"

"He's going out on another mission. I want you and Lang to meet me at the warehouse tonight at eight o'clock."

Hanging up, Dotsero allowed himself ten minutes to fully appreciate how easily life could become so complex. Then he had orders cut for one Zackary Johnson. About four o'clock that afternoon, Harkness showed up at his office door.

"I thought I told you that I would meet you later."

"Yeah, I know, but it really doesn't matter."

"Why?"

"Because Lang was found at the warehouse. He's dead, head damn near cut off and the money gone. I'll lay you five to one it was Johnson."

"Then he dies. I'll make sure that his dust off gets fucked up."

"I don't know... that's murder. I mean drugs are one thing, murder is quite another."

"Listen, you gutless bastard. He can put both of us away for a long time, not to mention the fact that because of that moral son-of-a-bitch we've lost the next shipment and the majority of our funding with it." Dotsero paused thoughtfully. "Anyway it's not really murder. It's war and the VC are going to kill him, not us."

They both rotated back to the States before they could recoup their losses. The only redeeming thought had been one of Zackary Johnson rotting in the jungle somewhere to the north. The sound of people arriving for work jarred Harkness out of his reverie.

Well, he thought, no time like the present. Pushing his bulk up out of his chair, he made his way through a chorus of 'Good mornings' from his staff and out into the hall. Turning left, he proceeded down the corridor to Colonel Dotsero's office. Walking into the outer office, he approached the Colonel's secretary. The small blond woman looked up from her typing. "Good morning, Chief Master Sergeant Harkness."

"Good morning, Nancy. Is the old man in? It's important that I see him."

"Yes, just a moment and I'll see if he can see you." Pressing the button on her intercom, she said, "Chief Master Sergeant Harkness is here to see you, sir. He says it's important."

"Send him in."

"You may go in."

"Thank you."

Walking into the inner office, Harkness closed the door behind him and turned toward the man sitting behind the massive oak desk. He couldn't make out any facial features walking toward him across the thick carpet. The window behind the desk, backlit the figure hunched over a thick sheaf of papers. Without looking up, Dotsero said, "What's so damned important?"

"Well Jason, does the name Zackary Johnson mean anything to you?"

Dotsero jerked erect, slamming his palm to the desktop and scattering papers.

"What the hell are you talking about? You know as well as I do that he must be dead."

"That's what I thought too, until last night when I saw him at The Hacienda having dinner with a cute young thing."

Dotsero visibly paled and jerked upright on his chair. "Did he see you?"

"No, I ducked back out while they were distracted by last night's storm. I waited in the parking lot until they came out and then followed him back to his motel."

Colonel Jason Dotsero eased his lean body back into his swivel chair and pushed a suddenly fatigued hand through his short-cropped silver hair. His washed-out blue eyes fixed Harkness with a weary stare. "Well, Chuck. It seems our work is cut out for us."

"What are you talking about? He can't touch us. There's no evidence."

"I'm not talking legalities. He must have found out about the setup and he's come back to even up the score."

"He still can't prove anything."

"Don't be simple, Chuck. He doesn't want to prove anything. He came here to kill us."

"Kill us? Don't you think that's a bit much?"

"We left that man to die. What would you do? I mean if you had the nerve?"

Harkness glowered at Dotsero for a moment and then dropped his gaze. Dotsero was right. Ever since Lang's death, he had been afraid. Who wouldn't be? Anyone who could kill like Zack had was not really human. Not human at all.

"I want you to tail him, find out why he's here. Then we can make plans."

Nodding in agreement, Harkness left the office without another word.

Chapter Seven

Pam awoke early the next morning. As was her custom since her mother's death and the need for an early rising, she stretched long and luxuriously and then snuggled down under the comforter. Her first conscious thought was of last night's dinner and how much she had enjoyed Zack's company.

She thought of him occasionally after she had gotten over that stupid schoolgirl crush. Ten had been a very hard year for her. She heard of him through her brother from time to time, but after a while, the family lost track. The last contact of any sort had been the arrival of a graduation card of congratulation in 1965. By then, Zackary was little more than a distant memory.

Well, last night all the memories came back, and to her surprise, a lot of the feelings returned. Not the feelings of a ten-year-old but of a full-grown woman. He seemed to be the same but changed somehow. He was older, of course, but the change was inside. He had a reserved air about him, not cold or unfeeling but more of a tendency to keep himself excluded from life.

Still lying in that hazy space between sleep and wakefulness, where thoughts drifted more than formed, she realized she had been very talkative during dinner, but he shared very little of himself. No, that wasn't quite true. He had been very open about his college days and then his work as a freelance writer since his return from Viet Nam. Coming fully awake, it dawned on her it was the Nam years he had not spoken about. She had read a few magazine articles on returning Nam Vets and some of the difficulties they faced when returning to civilian life. He didn't seem to fit into any of the categories she had heard or read about. She was curious but decided not to ask. Surely, he would bring it up if and when he was ready to talk about it. Something else struck her. She enjoyed his company because he listened to her. He really had. When she had started talking about her brother and his death, he held her hand and listened to her pain without turning away; a fine and valuable asset in a human being.

Lying there, she began to try and evaluate what she was really feeling. There was a definite sense of excitement. She was excited because he was a fresh face in a town so small that fresh faces were few and far between. Or was it that he was an old friend? Or was it a combination of the two?

She finally decided that she knew two things. One, she was attracted to him, and two, his arrival jarred her into the realization that she had been marking time for the last five years. She put off going to college for two years while her mother was dying from cancer. Her brother's death followed on the heels of her mother's funeral. That had been the last of her family. There was no good reason to stay on afterward. She just couldn't seem to get up enough energy to go. It occurred to her then how one day could blend into the next. How the sameness could be as mind-numbing as the most powerful psychotropic drug. Not that it had to be that way, but how easily you could let it become that way. If you were not responsible for your own life, then life would take the responsibility for you. The only problem was when that happened, the choices of life were probably not the choices that you had in mind. Pursuing the same line of thought, she suddenly realized why none of her post-high school relationships had been successful. She let others dictate and live her life for her instead of living it for herself. The realization reminded her of something she heard once: that age was really an acronym that stood for Another Growth Experience. Getting out of bed, she resolved to do two things. First, to develop a plan of action for herself and to act on it before the end of summer. Second, to sell the sporting goods store.

Chapter Eight

1972 Bangkok, Thailand

He wasn't a big man as men go. More average in height and build with blond collar-length hair set atop a broad fair-skinned forehead. Intelligent clear blue eyes gazed in weary resignation at the crowd of vehicles and pedestrian traffic stretched out before his Land Rover in the late afternoon sun. The road he was trying to negotiate was indeed wide enough to accommodate the normal flow of traffic, it had been originally designed for. However, the added pressure of the war combined with its tremendous influx of refugees together with their worldly possessions choked the roadways to a virtual standstill. The southern part of the city was the hardest hit. It was still very hard to find this degree of human flotsam in the north of the town with its broad boulevards lined with palm trees and fine old homes from the French colonial days.

Pulling up in front of a heavy wooden gate just off the main road, he blew his horn three short blasts followed by one long. The gate swung inward and he was waved through by a heavily armed local who promptly swung the gate shut, dropping a heavy crossbar in place.

Canyon of Death

The courtyard he found himself in was surrounded on three sides by the blank second story walls of the businesses to the left, right and behind him. The wall fronting the street side was solid, with the exception of the teak door. There was concertina wire stretched across the top of the wall and a sentry box built of armor plate stood at each corner.

In past years, this had been a warehouse for industrial machinery. They were still using it as a warehouse, but now where heavy machinery had once stood, every nook and cranny was filled to the rooftop with medicines, canned goods, blankets, bandages, powdered milk, case upon case upon case. The courtyard was choked with fuel drums and delivery vans. He was able to find a place to squeeze the Land Rover into and after shutting off the engine, he paused to survey the goods surrounding him. A conservative estimate placed their value somewhere around five hundred thousand U.S. dollars. He again marveled at how the whole thing had mushroomed.

He resigned his commission the previous year and decided to stay in-country. It had started on the evening of his one-month celebration of unemployment. He had been to one of the frequent cocktail parties that he infrequently attended. It was ironic that he chose to attend this one instead of passing it by as he usually did.

That was where he had met Patsy. A big rawboned woman who moved through the government/military crowd with a no-nonsense attitude demanding that someone pay attention to the plight of the orphaned children. He found her later in the evening sitting alone in the garden. Pausing just within the periphery of her vision, he lit a cigarette. She had glanced at the flick of his lighter. "Good evening." He acknowledged her greeting with an offer for a cigarette. "No, thank you."

"That was quite a performance you put on in there."

She looked at him like he was possibly one level above plant life. "That was no performance. If the U.S. government as well as the governments of all the other nations involved in this screwed-up mess don't start paying attention to what is happening with the orphaned by-products of this war, there is going to be one hell of a price paid in human suffering. No one seems to give a damn about any of the orphans, let alone the Amerasians which are starting to become a real problem and are the sole result of the U.S. involvement. Doesn't a nation that elects to become involved in a foreign war owe some sort of moral responsibility to the products of that involvement? Or is it considered acceptable to merely intervene and then walk away leaving the results of your intervention behind?"

Perry stood there with a look of surprise.

"I'm sorry. It's just that when I get started on that issue I have a hard time stopping."

He walked over and extended his hand. "John Perry." She accepted it and replied, "Patsy Walker."

She explained the work she was doing with the orphans under the auspices of the Peace Corps. They talked through most of the night and by the time they were through, he agreed to help her deliver some powdered milk to an outlying area the following day. It soon became evident that the entire distribution system was about as corrupt as it could get and still hoped to have any chance of functioning. He started dealing with the black marketers on a small-time basis, and before long, it grew to this. He sighed as he climbed down from the Land Rover and headed into his small office. Well, at least the kids were getting what they needed and no one was being hurt in the process.

The late afternoon, mail brought a welcome interruption to an otherwise long and frustrating day; a letter from Zack Johnson.

Although it had been three years since they had seen each other, they still kept in touch through the mail and with an occasional phone call. His mind drifted back to their last meeting. It had been in early July in the special wing of the base hospital in Da Nang,

South Viet Nam. This was his first visit to the hospital and he was surprised at the level of security present. After showing his ID and submitting himself to several minutes of scrutiny by the guard at the door, he was passed through into the interior. The nurse on duty told him that Zack was in room 115, which was just down the hall, turn left at the corner, and it would be on the right. It was hard to believe that Zack was alive. The section notified the previous afternoon that a chopper on routine patrol picked him up on the Thai side of the border with Laos, emaciated, racked with dysentery, and suffering from a variety of bruises and lacerations. The only other thing he learned was that Zack had been working his way toward friendly territory since escaping some two months previously.

Standing outside room 115, he took a deep breath and pushed the door open.

Zack lay on white sheets made all the whiter by his skin, still coated by jungle grime in contrast. They tried to clean him up, but the dirt that remained would take several days of steaming baths before it could be coaxed out. That was to say the visible skin was dirty, and there wasn't much visible above the sheet which covered him from the shoulders down.

"Jesus, you look awful."

Zack opened his eyes and looked at John. He could see the mirth dancing behind this friend's eyes. He hadn't changed much. The blond hair was a bit longer and he was now wearing a non-regulation mustache.

"Thank God. I'd hate to feel this way and look good."

They talked about Zack's capture, followed by almost two years of internment and eventual escape.

"I'll never forget that day. They brought the evening meal. At that time, I was the only one they were holding. The guard unlocked the door on the tiger cage I was being held in and yes, they were small. He pushed the food at me and closed the door, but didn't lock it. I sat and stared at that door for hours after the camp settled down for the night. I couldn't figure out what they were up to. When the sentry seemed to doze off, I decided to risk it. I spent two hours working my way out of that place. It felt like two days. I made it into the jungle and put several miles between me and them by daylight. I'd about had it by the time that chopper spotted me. I didn't find out how close I'd come until they picked me up. Seems they were under orders to bring back prisoners or they would have wasted me. The door gunner told me that dressed in the clothes I had on, wearing the coolie hat and standing in that elephant grass I looked just like a VC. They told me that the one thing that didn't make sense was my standing there waving at them. They thought it was a trap and almost didn't risk trying to 'capture' me."

John visited as often as he could during the month before Zack's discharge and rotation back to the States. During that time, they grew close despite their mutual aversion to closeness in a combat zone. It was the last visit before the subject of the dust-off came up.

John asked Zack, "What was it you were going to tell me about when I brought your order just before that last mission?"

Zack told him then of killing Lang and his confrontation with Dotsero and Dotsero's reaction.

"I think you were set up."

"What do you mean? By who?"

"Dotsero."

"That's pretty unlikely, he didn't have anything to do with that last operation. I was operating under Stienspring's control."

"No, you weren't, those orders came from Dotsero."

"How can you be sure?"

"I was on duty the morning of your extraction, monitoring radio traffic. Your chopper pilot was over the exact coordinates for your extraction. He reported you as a 'no show' and after ten minutes, he hauled ass. I talked to him when he returned to base and he told me he was positive he was at the right spot, the exact coordinates given to him by Dotsero. I didn't think too much of it at the time. I mean there could have been a variety of reasons that Steinspring turned your mission over to Dotsero. But, now think about it for a minute, if you were Dotsero and you had this 'little problem' what better way to take care of it? He knew that you couldn't evade it forever, especially after killing someone with that much power and influence. I think he gave the wrong coordinates and hoped you would disappear."

Zack didn't say anything. He just sat there staring off into the distance and at that moment John was very glad that he wasn't Jason Dotsero.

Chapter Nine

John received a letter from Zack shortly after Zack's return to the States. In it, Zack tried to explain his continued disillusionment with the war. He realized that he came into this as a wide-eyed innocent, and though he had recognized that the war jaded him somewhat, he still had been able to follow orders and carry out his assignments. He reasoned this from the viewpoint that, "They, the communists, were the enemy." Now, he was just no longer sure whose enemies 'they' were. He did know that they were not the enemies of his country and he had begun to doubt that they were the enemies of the people of South Viet Nam. In fact, he was beginning to suspect 'they' were the enemy of the corrupt political ruling power of South Viet Nam and the local citizenry be damned. He had also seen another thing clearly and that was, no matter who ruled in places such as this, it was the local citizen who suffered. The politicians and aristocratic class always told them they must suffer for their own good when in fact they suffered for the good of everyone else, rarely their own. He went on to explain that it was this line of reasoning that led him to resign his commission and return to civilian life.

There had been a smattering of mail between them since then. John kept up to date on Zack's new career as a freelance journalist and his continuing difficulties with Julie. Zack witnessed, through letters, John's disenchantment with the U.S. government's thoroughly screwed-up involvement in all of Southeast Asia, and John's final disillusionment resulted in the resignation of his commission. The one big difference was in the choice of paths taken, for while Zack returned to the States, John stayed in Southeast Asia. He told Zack of his true love of the region, the kindness of its people, the lushness of the jungles, the beauty of the Buddhist temples, and the sheer vitality that only day-to-day living can convey.

Zack also learned that John finally understood that it was the immediacy of life which truly attracted him. It didn't really matter much whether life could end by a bullet or starvation. What he discovered meant most to him, and that was, only by living life in the moment could he truly experience the vitality and harshness of it.

For the people who had the false security of health plans, unions, retirement, and a weekly paycheck, either by choice or accident, he felt only sadness. They would never experience the rich fabric of a full life that could only be theirs by casting off the very aspects of life that were touted as security. When, in fact, this false security brought about a complacency that was only shackles that bound more completely than the strongest chains.

A long blast of a truck's horn intruded on his thoughts. He slit the flap of the envelope with his teak-handled letter opener.

The letter began.

Dear John, 31 June 1972

By the time this reaches you, I should be in New Mexico. I received a very odd letter from my father's executor last week. In it, my dad told a strange story of finding what he believed to be the location of some lost Spanish gold. Do you remember that story I told you that night in Udorn? I only half believed it myself but now that I have a map and some sketchy directions, I'm going to try and find it.

I could use some help. All I can offer is a share in anything that we may find. If you're interested you can reach me at (505) 555-6781. Hope to hear from you soon.

It was signed by Zack.

John sat there for a while thinking that he really should take a vacation. It would be great to see Zack again and an adventure was just what he needed to break the cycle of frustration he was feeling.

He booked himself on the next flight out of Bangkok International to Albuquerque, New Mexico, via New York's JFK. He then called the number that Zack gave him and found Zack to be out until the following day. He left a message with his arrival time and hung up.

*****

Canyon of Death

Zack backed into the parking slot in front of his motel room. Deciding first things first, he went into the bathroom before unpacking. He was on his way out when he noticed the message light on his phone blinking. Rather than calling the desk, he decided to go over to the office and check on it in person before he unloaded the Scout.

Walking across the asphalt parking lot, he became aware of the heat as it seeped through the soles of his boots. The sky was a hazy blue with a few clouds that sat puffy white on the mountain ranges off to the west. The rains were late this year. By now, the rainy season should be in full swing.

The little motel office was icy cold as the result of a window air conditioning unit laboring with a thudding and clanging noise that made conversation difficult, if not impossible. He was greeted by an excited desk clerk.

"Never seen the like of it," exclaimed the dour old man.

"What are you talking about?"

"That phone call."

"What phone call?"

"The one you got."

This exchange was starting to become pretty exasperating to Zack until he realized that this particular call if it was from who he thought it was, was probably the most exciting call that the old man ever received. He decided to take a deep breath and let him enjoy his moment.

"And what would that one be?"

"Oh, oh, here you are," and so saying he passed the message to Zack.

"I just can't believe it, all the way from Bangkok, Thailand. I've never been that far. Hell, I've only been out of the state twice and then only to El Paso for a few days. Had me some family over there once. Didn't visit a regular though." Thanking the man, Zack picked up the message and left the clerk to his ceaseless rambling, waiting until he re-crossed the sunbaked asphalt of the parking lot and entered the machine-controlled atmosphere of his air-conditioned motel room before looking at the phone message which read: "Zack, I am arriving in Albuquerque on Delta #346 at 10:00 a.m. on Sunday the 19th of July." Signed John.

Zack was pleased and grateful that John was coming. He was pleased because John meant more to him as a friend than he cared to admit and grateful, for without John, his embryonic plan had little hope of success. On his way back into town, he had concluded that for this venture to have a half-assed chance to succeed, he would need the help of at least one companion. Someone strong and willing to do grunt work, due to the sheer weight of gold to be moved. Someone whom he could trust implicitly. And now he had that.

Zack stripped off his boots, travel-stained Levi's, shirt, shorts, and socks and padded barefoot into the bathroom for a long hot shower to prepare for tonight's date with Pam.

Chapter Ten

It was early evening by the time Zack was dressed and ready to leave. He still had about an hour before he was supposed to pick Pam up. Too keyed up to sit in the motel room and wait, he decided to just drive around and sort out some things. One of which was why he wanted to see Pam again, and what he wanted from her. When he finally pulled up in front of her house, he had concluded that all he wanted, right now, was an enjoyable female companion to share some good conversation with over a decent meal. Walking up the well-tended brick path to her front door, he was struck by how much he had missed the sight and smell of traditional adobe. The reddish mud plaster had a rich warm glow as it reflected the fading rays of the setting sun from its western wall. The spacious windows nestled under the thatched roof of the western-facing porch also reflected the sun's setting rays. The doors and windows were all framed in wood and painted in a traditional turquoise, a color chosen to represent water, which was always in short supply. Taking a deep breath of the rich earthy smell of the home, he was struck by the faint subtle fragrance wafting from the garden nestled on the south side of the house, which he now noticed for the first time. Looking at its riot of color, he reflected on the immense variety of flowers unknown to him. He then lifted the heavy brass door knocker and let it fall onto the brass plate affixed to the heavy oak door with its black wrought iron strap hinges.

The echo of the single knock was beginning to die away when Pam opened the door.

"Come in, won't you? I'll just be a minute." As she disappeared into the rear of the house, she called over her shoulder, "Help yourself to anything in the fridge if you want to."

Zack walked across the tiled floor through the living room with its low wooden couches covered with cushions upholstered in an Indian blanket-type fabric in a design comprised of reds and grays. He stopped once to admire a large abstract painting of a canyon. Its vivid colors brought the interior, whitewashed adobe bricks to life. The use of colors was very compelling and leaning closer, he noted the artist's name, Carol Hoy. Entering the kitchen, he was struck by the modern stainless-steel design complete with fluorescent lighting set into a recessed ceiling which had replaced the traditional open vega design evident elsewhere in the house. In fact, the only acknowledgment of tradition in this room was in the countertops, which had been done in four-inch square hand-painted Mexican tile. He pulled a cold Pepsi from amidst the mix of beer and soft drinks available and returned to the living room to await Pam.

"Well, I'm ready."

"Let's do it."

They decided to head over to Silver City for a casual dinner at one of the steak houses. Watching Pam precede him to his truck, he automatically responded to the sway of her Levi's clad bottom. There was something undeniably sexy about a well-proportioned female in cowboy boots and Levi's.

The drive over was pleasant. They talked of mutually shared memories. Pam spoke more of her mother's death and how the store, which had been left to her, was becoming more of a burden than an asset. However, the drive was spent mostly in companionable silence. They were shown to a table against the wall by a hostess clad in a full-length gingham dress. Placing their drink orders, a glass of house red for Pam and a Chivas rocks for him, they turned to study the room. The dining room resembled a dining room one would expect to find in a large private home rather than a public restaurant. The floor was covered in thick carpet of emerald green in a floral pattern. There were several old antique oak pieces scattered about, including sideboards, ice boxes, and china cabinets. The light coming from above was supplied by crystal chandeliers converted to electricity. The wait staff was dressed in western garb as were the majority of the patrons. The women wore denim, either jeans or skirts, topped by western shirts or ruffled blouses and boots while their male companions seemed to favor, almost without exception, cowboy boots, Levi's, western shirts and a bolo tie of some fashion.

Their waiter unobtrusively placed their drinks before them and withdrew. Zack raised his glass to Pam.

"To old friends."

Pam acknowledged the toast and they both drank.

"How's the research going?"

"Fine. I was down in the Gila Wilderness yesterday. My dad used to lease grazing rights out there before the war. I wanted to see what the usage by the small ranchers was and also to talk to them about any problems they might be having. Nothing real specific, just some general background. How have things been going for you?"

The conversation continued in this light and uncomplicated vein as they worked their way through a good steak dinner. It was over dessert and coffee that it turned to a more serious note when Pam said, "Zack, is it OK if I ask you some questions about Viet Nam? Freddie hadn't really written home that often and you are the only vet I feel I know well enough to ask. What was it like?"

He paused for a moment to try and sort through the swirl of emotion the question caused. He took a sip of coffee and lit another Camel. Laying his battered Zippo lighter on the table beside the half-

73

crushed pack of cigarettes, he took a deep slow breath and let it out slowly.

He began to speak in his deep voice and as he did so he began playing with his lighter while his gaze drifted to some unfocused spot on the ceiling.

"Well, first of all, it would depend on which Viet Nam war you were in. It was very different in that respect. The war of the 18-year-old river rat on patrol in the Mekong Delta wasn't much different from the 18-year-old grunt in the bush, but they were both worlds apart from the air crews who were on the average much older and for the most part 'committed' to the war. The kids fought a more intimate war in the raw filth of the bush while the air crews fought a more insular war in the pristine air. Then you had the guys like me. The fringe characters, spooks as we were often called in-country. The correct word is assassin. By the way, did you know that the term assassin was coined in the 11th century to describe a group of fanatical Ismailis who operated in Persia and Syria as a secret order and who considered their murders to be a religious duty? Anyway, I can only answer your question from my perspective. When I completed my first kill, I felt good. Good because I had done what I had been trained to do and I had gotten out alive. It wasn't until much later that I realized that I was becoming emotionally dead. You see, the 'founding fathers' of my profession had their religious belief system to sustain them in their chosen line of work while I and others like me were selected by our government to perform this function based on the government's belief system rather than on our own. Before long, there was nothing left on the inside. I tried to rationalize that to be able to use a scoped sniper's rifle, to watch a target's head explode, with no other feeling than cold competence was a laudable thing. I mean, 'they' were the enemy. I will never forget the day, full of horror of what was happening to me, hit home. You see, the human animal can live through some of the most horrific circumstances and evidence little outward emotional damage. And then one day a benign experience will have the most significant impact. I was walking through a downtown section of Udorn, Thailand when I came upon a large group of street children. Before I was aware of what was happening, they were all around me. Whenever and wherever I looked down I saw their distended bellies, swollen from malnutrition, a sea of soft brown eyes gazing back at me, outstretched hands, too beaten by war and life to even whisper. Their eyes implored the silent question, 'food G.I., food?' I was overwhelmed by their sheer number and the hopelessness of it all. And then, I realized that I could only feed a handful and besides that,

I didn't really give a damn. So, I pushed on through them, shaking off the few who clung to me, and moved on.

Sometimes I think that the ones like Freddie, or the ones who have visible physical or obvious psychological wounds, are in some ways luckier than the ones who came back as detached observers. I'm not even sure if detached observer is the right expression. It's as close as I can come to describe the emptiness inside. It's almost as if after you realize that you can be dead in a second, you begin to try and cram all of the remaining fifty or sixty years of a normal life into the period of the war, which you are convinced you are not going to live through. Then, when you do, how do you 'decompress' this span so you can live a full life? Anyway, I and others are functioning observers. Observers who cause no trouble or burden for society, contribute to the GNP but may never be willing or able to expose that very private part of their inner core which is all that they have left. You have to understand that they have given all that they can and still be able to function. If they lose that last part of themselves, they will snap. I know that I learned the loneliness of my soul to survive that madness. I just don't know if I will ever be willing or able to return to being involved with life or if I will continue as a detached observer. I do know, in my heart, that I will never trust my government. I love my country but I wouldn't give you two cents for the majority of politicians. Ah, what the hell. I didn't mean to dump all that but then again, you are the only one who has ever asked. It always seemed to me that people didn't want to talk about it. It was over, so forget about it, don't bother others with your pain, and in doing so, bring attention to their pain."

He found it comfortable to tell Pam about it. Not intending to tell her so much, he found himself going on and on, the more he said, the easier it was to say more.

"Pain?"

"Yes."

"There is something else," Zack paused, lit another cigarette and continued. "I've never told anyone this much about my feelings before and I've never admitted to the one thing which still bothers me."

Pam sat quietly waiting for him to continue. "I miss it. I still do! For all of the misery and agony, there was a feeling of being intensely alive and I haven't found that since."

Pam's face had taken on a look of total acceptance of his humanness. It was so open that Zack dropped his eyes. "I'm sorry," his voice was a hoarse whisper, "to have dumped like that on you."

"You don't have to apologize. I asked you what it was like. Thank you for telling me. Do you know what I think?"

"No."

"Do you want to?"

"Yes."

"I think that for you to talk about it the way you did is the first step in healing your wounds. Are you ready to go?"

Chapter Eleven

Harkness called Dotsero and left word on his answering machine to meet at a bar in Las Cruces called The Outpost on Saturday any time after 1:00 p.m. Dotsero met Harkness at the nondescript bar on the south side of Las Cruces that early Saturday afternoon. Walking inside, Dotsero paused, allowing his eyes to adjust from the bright glare of the sun to the dim interior. He let his eyes drift over the early drinkers sitting at the stained bar, their beer and whiskey sitting in front of them as they leaned on their elbows with the weight of life hanging from their shoulders. Finally, he spotted the beefy man in a booth in the far corner at the back. He stopped at the bar for a cold Coors, walked back, and slid onto the bench seat. He nodded a greeting to Harkness, took a long swallow, placed the bottle in front of him, and said, "What did you find out?"

"I nosed around like you wanted me to and I got lucky. Johnson left his motel early the morning after you and I first talked. When I drove by, his truck was gone, so I decided to take a chance and went in to see the clerk, a real old gabby guy. I told him I'd seen this guy getting into an old Scout parked in front of room six this morning on my way to work and it looked a little like an old war buddy of mine. Well, the more I thought about it, the more curious I became, so I decided to come back to find out but he was gone. Well, anyway, this old guy tells me the guy's name and that he was a freelance writer checking on big conglomerates buying up small ranches. He was also wondering if I knew another guy named John seeing as how John was a friend of Mr. Johnson's and he was flying into Albuquerque on Sunday at 10:00 a.m. on Delta. He was waving this phone message in my face the whole time he was talking. I acted really excited and said that I knew both of them. Then I asked him if Mr. Johnson was coming back and he said, yeah he'd be back on Friday. I told him that I wanted to surprise both of them but I wanted to get a few other friends together first and gave him a twenty to keep quiet. I waited until after Johnson left this morning and then called his motel. The guy told me that I had missed him, that Mr. Johnson checked out and wouldn't be back and no, he hadn't said a word. I thanked him, hung up, and called you."

"Good. I want you to get up to Albuquerque and do two things. Meet the Delta flight, find out who this John is, and then tail them both. Call me Sunday night and report. In the meantime, I'll put you on two weeks of emergency leave effective Monday morning. Now, let's get out of this dump."

Chapter Twelve

Zack pulled out of the motel parking lot at daybreak on Saturday morning. The dawn air was cool and crisp, belying the intense temperatures to come later in the day. The sky was light blue and clear without a hint of rain, which was normal for this time of year.

Glancing at his watch, he quickly computed the driving time to Albuquerque and figured he would get there about the time the library opened. He wanted to research any possible known information about the gold shipment before John's arrival the following morning. He stopped for breakfast at Belen and hit the Central I-25 off-ramp just before 9:00 a.m. Proceeding west to 5th Street, he turned north to the parking lot adjacent to the library and walked in just as they opened.

A cursory check on Maximilian surprised him as to how little he knew of him, beyond the fact that he had been emperor of Mexico. Limiting his investigation to the last year of rule, he found that in 1865, a chain of events was set in motion when the United States demanded Napoleon to withdraw his troops. After the troops were withdrawn, Maximilian was captured and shot following a court martial by Juarez in 1867.

Although he spent most of Saturday at both the public library and the Zimmerman library on campus at the University of New Mexico, he could find no specific proof of any gold being shipped out of Mexico during that time. The most he could come up with was a book on legends concerning lost treasures in the southwest United States. There was one brief chapter devoted to a wagon train consisting of ten supply wagons, heavily loaded, and a complement of twenty French soldiers under the command of a young French officer. The wagon train headed north from Mexico City sometime in early March 1867. These wagons were rumored to carry 5,000–6,000 pounds of gold bullion aboard. There wasn't any further mention of where they were heading or if they had reached their destination.

Zack pulled his notepad, did some quick rough calculations, and figured that if this account was valid, at today's market value, there was some $18,000,000 to $21,000,000 worth of gold that was gone missing somewhere.

He ate lunch at the Frontier, an off-campus restaurant that he hadn't frequented since his college days. The food was excellent, as usual. After finishing up at the library, he spent the remainder of the afternoon at a sporting goods store picking up camping gear for John and a topographical map of the Gila Wilderness. He then wandered around Old Town, visiting some of his favorite shops. He was pleased at how little things had changed since his undergraduate days. The people were still friendly, the shop owners as well as the sidewalk vendors with their native American jewelry spread on blankets below the outdoor porch of the La Hacienda. He finished off the day with an early dinner at La Hacienda. It was one of his favorite restaurants, both for their chile rellenos and their decor. The restaurant was originally one of the first homes when Albuquerque was founded in 1706 by Francisco Cuervo Yvaldes.

Leaving the restaurant, he followed Central East to southbound I-25 and backtracked to his hotel. He chose the AmFac due to its proximity to the airport and in a few minutes, he exited at Gibson, turned east to Yale, then south to the hotel.

He checked in and spent the remainder of the evening in his room compiling his notes and comparing his father's map to the top of the Gila Wilderness. As close as he could figure it, he and John were headed for Diamond Peak in the Gila Primitive Area. At almost 9,000 feet, it promised to be an interesting trip, to say the least. He finished up his notes about things he wanted to tell John and turned in for the evening.

Chapter Thirteen

Zack was sitting in Delta's arrival lounge by 8:00 a.m. the next morning. There were few travelers about and he had no problem finding three seats in a row by the window, allowing him plenty of room to enjoy his cup of coffee while he spread out the Sunday morning edition of the *Albuquerque Journal*.

He was struck by the sense of Deja vu as he scanned the pages; gang problems, DWIs, corruption in state and county politics, contaminated groundwater, trouble with the Albuquerque school system, and ongoing concerns with the public utilities. It seemed as if nothing had changed since he left seven years ago. He saved the best part of the paper for the last, the comics. He had done that since childhood. Like the way he still saved the cherry from a hot fudge sundae, anticipation was always more fun than the event.

He timed it just right, finishing his paper and a third cup of coffee as they announced the arrival of John's flight.

John, having treated himself to first class, was one of the first off. Stepping out of the stream of passengers, the two men embraced, exchanged greetings, and turned toward the baggage claim area. After claiming John's luggage, they stopped for brunch at one of the restaurants near the airport. The conversation remained light, by mutual unspoken agreement, through the meal. It wasn't until they were southbound on I-25 that John broke a comfortable silence.

"Well, my friend, would you mind telling me what's going on and where are we going?"

Zack glanced over at his friend and passing him a buff colored file folder, said, "Why don't you read this. It's all the info I've been able to gather so far. Then we'll talk."

As John started to read, they entered a light shower and drove on, the silence was broken only by the periodic swish of the wipers set on mist setting. After the better part of an hour, John dropped the closed file on the seat between them. Taking a pack of Camels from his shirt pocket, he shook out a cigarette from the slightly dented pack. After offering one to Zack, which was refused, he tapped the unfiltered smoke against his Zippo and lit it. He cracked the window a bit to better vent the smoke. Raising his voice above the noise of the outside slipstream, he said, "That's quite a story. Do you agree with your father's assumption that something is buried in that tunnel and that something is the fabled lost gold shipment?"

Zack looked thoughtfully out through the rain-spattered windshield before replying. "I'm not sure, I think so. I mean, all the pieces I've gathered seem to point in that direction. I've been trying to figure out if I do believe him, and if I do, why? Is it because of the money or the fact that a man I never knew, my father, has left something for me, or is it because it's an unfinished job that my father wants finished and I'm somehow responsible for completing it?"

"You forgot one other possibility."

"What's that?"

"The sheer adventure of it!"

"You're right, there's that."

"So, as I said earlier, where are we going?"

"I've reserved a room for us in Silver City for tonight and then we are going on a backpacking trip into the Gila Wilderness. I figure we'll be gone for about a week. In that time, we should be able to find out if there's anything to this or not."

"How much company can we expect?"

"What are you talking about?"

"How many other backpackers, hikers, campers, and so forth can we expect to run into?"

"Not many. The Gila is not normally used by many people and the usage really drops off at this time of year because of the rainy season, which is late by the way."

They reached Silver City in the early evening and on the way to their motel stopped and picked up a large pizza with everything and

Canyon of Death

a six pack of Heineken dark. After checking in, they deposited their gear in the room and proceeded to attack the pizza, washing it down with a beer apiece. Clearing away the empty box and opening a second bottle each, they spread out the topo map and began planning their trip into the target area.

Chapter Fourteen

Harkness sat in the cramped front seat of the rental car. All that had been available was a Ford Escort and it didn't even come close to accommodating his bulk. His hastily eaten dinner of two burritos lay like a rock in the pit of his stomach. The gas was already beginning to move through his lower intestine like a mouse sneaking through a tunnel; move, pause, move. He had to piss so badly, his head hurt. He checked his watch for the hundredth time. It seemed as if he had been sitting there for days when in actuality it had been only five hours. He pulled a tired hand down his sagging face. Were they ever going to turn off the fucking lights?

It was just past midnight when the lights finally did go out. Harkness heaved a sigh of relief as he started his car and wound his way through the nearly deserted streets to his motel on the other side of town. It was past 2 a.m. when he called Dotsero in Las Cruces. The connection was made after the fifth ring.

"Uh."

"Jason?"

"Yeah. Who's this?"

"Chuck."

He felt the man at the other end of the line snap into full wakefulness.

"Good, what have you got? Where are you?"

"I'm in Silver City. Johnson met the Delta flight in Albuquerque as scheduled. Remember John Perry? That chopper pilot Johnson was so tight with? Well, he was the one Johnson was waiting for. I followed them here and from the looks of the gear they unloaded, they were planning an extended backpacking trip. What do you want me to do now?"

"You stick to them. If they are on a backcountry trip, they will have to leave their vehicle at some trailhead somewhere. When they do, you call me." The line went dead.

Harkness depressed the button, dialed the front desk, and left a four-a.m. wake-up call. Hanging up, he was asleep before his head hit the pillow.

Chapter Fifteen

They turned off State Road 152 onto County Road 35, pulling over for a cup of coffee just before dawn. They stood beside the Scout drinking from the thermos they had filled at an all-night cafe on the outskirts of Silver City.

The early morning sun was just beginning to touch the peaks of the Black range. "Beautiful, isn't it?" commented Zack.

The sun was sending long pinkish fingers through the upper reaches of the Douglas Fir on the peaks, highlighting the underside of the early morning cloud cover. John stood mesmerized for a moment before he nodded in concurrence.

"What can you tell me about this area?"

"The little bit I remember came from some courses I took at UNM. This region was originally designated as the Gila Wilderness in 1924 largely through the efforts of a local forest ranger named Aldo Leopold. In 1933, an eastern section was withdrawn from the Wilderness Area and re-designated as the Gila Primitive Area. This re-designation allowed grazing permits to be issued. My father obtained one and grazed cattle here until the beginning of World War II. It's pretty well choked with side canyons. The lower slopes and canyon bottoms are predominately grassing with cottonwoods and Ponderosa pine while the upper slopes are mainly Aspen and Douglas Fir."

They finished their coffee, climbed back into the Scout, continued north by northwest to County Road 163, where they turned almost due north and continued to the Upper Black Canyon campground.

Harkness drove past them as they were starting to unload their gear. He continued north past Wall Lake, east on County Road 59 until he intercepted I-25 at Truth or Consequences, or Hot Springs as it was known until it was renamed for a famous radio show in the 50s.

John cast a baleful eye at the mound of equipment at his feet. "I'll bite, what and how? I've never been backpacking."

"OK, first things first. Let's pack our gear."

The packs they were using had an external frame design that supported a ripstop nylon pack consisting of two compartments, upper and lower, with zippered side compartments and two zippered pouches, one on the lower back facing to the outside and one on the top flap which pulled over the opening in the top of the upper compartment.

"The object is to keep the weight low on your body while at the same time keeping things like matches, water bottles, compass, maps, whistle, flashlight, and first aid kit handy. We'll split the commonly shared items. You take the tent and I'll take the cooking gear."

As John watched, Zack started on his pack placing the pack frame down on the ground. He placed the cooking gear — stove, pots, pans, cups, plates, and utensils — on the lower compartment of his pack, filling in the nooks and crannies with spices, tea, and coffee. After zipping the lower pouch shut, he stood it upright and leaned it against the Scout. He then began packing the upper compartment. He placed his clothing in first followed by dehydrated food. He then secured the flap, sealing the upper compartment and making it virtually waterproof. The butane fuel bottles, first aid kit, water bottles, flashlights, maps, and matches were stored in the various zippered compartments located on the outside of the pack. On top of the upper compartment, he secured his sleeping bag which was wrapped inside his Gortex sleeping pad. A lanyard with a whistle and compass slung around his neck completed the process.

John watched and followed Zack's movements with intense interest. As Zack looked over, John was just finishing up and was holding the tent with a questioning look. Zack secured it for him.

The two packs looked identical with the exception of the tent secured on top of John's pack with his sleeping bag and Gortex pad.

"Now," said Zack, "for the most important part, our feet."

Sitting down on the lowered tailgate, he pulled off his tennis shoes and socks. Next, he produced a packet of mole skin and a pair of small scissors which he used to cut the moleskin into various sizes and shapes.

"What is that stuff and what do you use it for?"

"You use it to protect the 'hot spots' your hiking boots cause when they chafe against your feet." Tossing a piece over to John, he said, "Look, one side is soft and fuzzy, kind of like a mole's skin. Hence the name. The other side has an adhesive. I know my hot spots are on the left heel and the right ankle in front. You can either guess at yours now and adjust later or go without for about a half mile. They should start showing up by then and we can stop so you can use the stuff."

Zack then covered his feet with a thin inner sock followed by a wool sock and then put on his hiking boots, lacing them up. After John finished with the same procedure, they helped each other into their backpacks, locked the Scout, and started north on 163 toward their jumping-off point at Diamond Creek.

The morning had dawned bright and clear but was beginning to cloud up by the time they reached the East Fork of Diamond Creek. The thunderheads were beginning to march in from the east and were starting to stack up along the upper ridges of the Black Range. By now, lightning was striking the upper peaks with regularity. The creek entrance was a narrow cut through the rock. The trail they chose followed the south bank of the stream. It climbed steadily for some time and showed fewer advantageous spots for a crossing that wasn't almost vertical. The worsening sky coupled with a vivid image of his first flash flood caused Zack to stop seeking a more opportune spot and to make the necessary crossing as soon as possible. He quickly led them down twenty feet of loose rock and gravel and then up the other side.

"What's the hurry?" asked John.

Zack pointed skyward, "Have you ever seen a flash flood?" John shook his head. "They aren't very pretty." He went back to his memories.

It happened when he was ten. He was helping his uncle move some cattle that spring from the ranch up to summer pasture. He was warned of the dangers associated with the dry arroyos, especially during spring runoff, but that morning, it was clear. The only clouds in sight were hugging the mountaintops to the west some 20 miles away. They couldn't possibly affect where he was, he reasoned, as he drove the ten head of cattle into the wide dry arroyo.

Besides, he would save several hours with the shortcut and beat everyone to the upper pastures. He would surely show them.

He moved for about an hour when the lead steer stopped and then started to try and climb the side of the arroyo. Moving to cut the steer off, his horse started to prance side to side. It was at that moment, the lead steer pivoted and stampeded back downhill with the rest of the herd in hot pursuit.

Zack heard it then, a low dull, roaring sound. His mount panicked and followed the cattle in a headlong plunge downhill away from the frightening noise that grew louder by the second. Zack, hanging on for all that he was worth, looked ahead and saw a thin, almost impossible cut in the high back leading off to the right. It looked almost vertical but it did present the only possible way out. The lead steer already passed it and as he drew abreast, he kneed his horse and pulled hard on his right rein. His mount swung hard and lunged up through the cut, pausing for a moment balanced on the edge, before carrying over onto firm ground.

He slid out of the saddle and looked below as the water swept past pushing trees, brush, and boulders as big as armchairs ahead of it. The water swept up the trailing steer and in the blink of an eye, it swallowed the whole herd.

It was late evening by the time he made camp and told his uncle what happened. His uncle hadn't said a word and Zack never did anything that stupid again.

The storm they were expecting never did break and by late afternoon, they reached the plateau his father's map showed. They made camp by the base of the cliff and by dusk, found the tunnel against the base of the cliff just as the map promised. It was a gaping hole approximately twelve feet wide by some ten feet high. Even as big as it was, it hadn't been easy to locate. The surrounding landscape altered quite a bit by both time and weather since its discovery by Zack's father some 30 years before. The saplings referred to as landmarks were now large trees and a lot of scrub brush had taken root, further disguising the entrance. They moved their campsite to the tunnel's mouth by moonlight and gratefully crawled into their sleeping bags.

Although neither man got much sleep, the predawn darkness found them both wide awake. The tunnel beckoned both of them through the night with unspoken promises of wealth, adventure, and excitement. When they rolled out of their sleeping bags, the early morning dawn was a thin band of grayish light providing a backdrop to the tops of the peaks to the east. It rained heavily the previous night and the sky was still producing a fine misty rain. The trees dripped with excess moisture and the cliff face gleamed wetly in the early morning light.

Working on their second cup of coffee, they continued to plan their course of action.

"From the little bit we were able to see last night," said John, "it would appear that we have a lot of rock to move."

"We might as well get to it. It isn't going to move itself. What do you think about hauling the loose stuff over to the edge and dropping it over the side? I don't want to risk discovery until we find out what's here."

"I agree. If there is anything here, we'll have to come back for it, so let's not leave any more clues than we have to. If there isn't anything, at least the exercise will do us some good."

They approached the mass of rock that effectively choked off the tunnel. Studying it, John began to trace a "V" image with his outstretched hands. Zack gave him an amused glance.

"What the hell are you trying to do, drive them away?"

"I was just thinking. We don't have to move all the rock, we just have to gain access to whatever is on the other side. Why don't we take it out beginning in the center and let the rock form a natural slope from the ceiling to the floor?"

"Let's give it a try."

They slogged through the day. Initial quips concerning the benefits of exercise soon gave way to wordless movement of endless repetition. Lift, turn, walk to the cliff edge and drop. By the end of the day, they were beyond caring for food and they dropped into their sleeping bags in a state of total exhaustion. They managed to clear out a small tunnel running from floor to ceiling. It was only some four feet wide at its base with gently sloping sides reaching up to the roof. Dawn of the second day found them hard at it.

The tunnel was going well. Their initial plan to remove only the rock required to gain access to whatever, if anything, that lay within was working.

The rock dust was becoming almost unbearable when John pulled out a football-sized rock jammed against the roof of the tunnel and was rewarded with a breath of fresh air.

"I'm through!"

"Can you see anything?"

John shone his flashlight through the opening and was able to make out dim bulky shapes but nothing of any substance or detail.

"Yes, but I can't make out what it is."

They attacked the remaining rock and within moments, they created an opening large enough so that they were able to tumble through into a large natural cavern.

Canyon of Death

As their eyes adjusted to the gloom, they were greeted by an awe-inspiring sight. In front of them, there were ten crumbling freight wagons. The wooden structures long ago surrendered to the effects of decomposition brought on by the combination of air, cargo weight, and moisture. Drawing closer to the wagons in the cathedral-like silence, they noted hundreds of wooden crates stacked within the wagons' remains. Several of the crates split open. A sudden shift of cloud cover momentarily exposed the sun, letting it shine through a natural opening in the roof of the cavern. The sunlight glinted dully off the gold bars that leaked out of one of the crates.

Chapter Sixteen

"Jesus, Jesus H. Christ," John said in a reverent tone. "Look at it. There must be millions here."

Zack looked at him as a slow smile slit his face. "If the myth is even fairly accurate there's about 5,000–6,000 pounds of it. At today's market value, that's between 18 and 21 million dollars' worth."

Slowly they wandered through the cavern, shining their flashlights on the old decrepit wagons. Pausing beside one, Zack placed his hand on a wheel, and with a groan, the wagon collapsed in slow motion.

Jumping back, Zack dusted off his hands and said, "Of course, we still have two minor problems. How are we going to get it out and how are we going to dispose of it?"

"Right. I hadn't thought about that. Hell, I didn't even think we would find anything. We sure can't take it out the way we came in."

"We may not have to."

"What have you got in mind?"

"Well, for starters, those wagons couldn't have come up that way either. There had to have been a trail wide enough to have handled that type of traffic in the past. Let's get out of here and look for it."

They found it late that afternoon. The trail, or what was left of it, led off from the east side of the mesa.

"Looks pretty rough from here," said Zack as he started down. "Let's hike it a bit and see what shape it's in."

"I don't think we can haul anything up here to take the gold out on; some of these cuts are pretty deep."

They turned a corner and were greeted with space. Zack turned to John. "You still have a current chopper rating, don't you?"

Over dinner that night, they formulated their plans as the thunder boomed and the lightning sizzled and cracked, striking the surrounding mountain peaks. The shower that struck later was brief but held a promise of the intensity waiting to vent itself upon the land.

Chapter Seventeen

It was late afternoon when he caught sight of them. The old tan Ford van with patches of blue and yellow paint showing through its brush-scraped sides pulled into the parking area below his vantage point. He honestly didn't know if he was happier because they finally returned, and the awful gut-wrenching days and nights of self-doubt were over, or because he wouldn't have to spend another night on this God-forsaken rock. Lord, he hated camping.

He took up his position after calling Dotsero from T or C. It had seemed reasonable, at the time, that they would return to the parked Scout but as one day turned to two and then three he had begun to have doubts.

He watched as Zack and John unloaded their backpacks and other gear and with a wave of thanks to the van's driver, they began to load the Scout.

Harkness quickly rolled up his sleeping bag and shelter, half jamming them into a large laundry bag which already held the balance of his meager gear, and got ready to follow them.

They pulled out from the parking area and turned south on 162. He was fifteen minutes behind them when he reached the main road and was faced with an east/west choice. He gambled and swung west toward Silver City. The gamble paid off when he spotted the Scout outside one of the first motels on the city's outskirts. Driving past, he checked into one of those cheaper motels available on the southern edges of most towns. Within minutes of checking in, he was holding an old-fashioned black Bakelight receiver to his ear as he dialed the number for Dotsero with his free hand. While listening to the ringing of the phone, Harkness noticed movement in the corner of the room. A cockroach was approaching from a small puddle of water that had formed under the air conditioner on the warped linoleum tile. He watched as it gained the edge of the threadbare mildewed carpet and continued toward him. Three events occurred in quick succession: he raised his foot to stomp the roach, the rump-sprung bed groaned in protest at the sudden movement and Dotsero answered.

Chapter Eighteen

The heavy early morning cloud cover was so thick sunrise occurred without any dramatically noticeable change. The sky just grew gradually lighter.

Harkness and Dotsero sat in a parking lot, across the street from Zack and John's motel, and waited. It was 8:15 a.m., 69F, 37C, according to the digital display on the clock outside the Sun west bank on the corner when Zack and John came out.

Zack started the Scout and was letting the engine warm up when John emerged from the motel office folding what looked like a room bill into the pocket of his denim shirt.

They followed them to a car rental agency in the center of town and when John got out so did Dotsero. Harkness followed Zack as he headed east.

During the previous night's discussions, they finally concluded that Zackary was totally ignorant of their presence. As incredible as it may seem, their being in the same place at the same time was coincidence.

As the night grew longer and the level of scotch continued to dwindle another possibility for Zack and John's presence in New

Mexico dawned on them. Harkness brought it up first. "Remember when Zack first got in-country?"

"No."

"Sure, you do. I told you all about it. How I overheard him and John talking in Mama Woo's place about his daddy's lost gold mine. Do you think that's why they're here?"

Dotsero sat up straighter and his eyes seemed to clear as he tried to shake off the effects of the night's drinking.

"It's just crazy enough to be possible."

They went on to further reason that they had two possible courses of action open to them. They could go home and forget the whole thing or they could follow Zack and John and try to find out what they were up to.

The first choice suggested the possibilities of loose ends, which Dotsero deplored, while the second plucked the strings of avarice on the heart of Harkness. They discussed the pros and cons of both choices for hours.

Finally, in the best interest of both, they chose the second course of action. They agreed that if Zack and John should separate for any reason, Harkness would stick with Zack while Dotsero followed John. If this situation should occur then they would communicate through the switchboard at their motel.

Sitting in a coffee shop across the street, Dotsero watched the front door of the rental agency through a grease-streaked window. It was close to 9:00 a.m. before John pulled out of the rental agency's parking lot driving the last subcompact in sight.

A few minutes later, Dotsero walked into the office. The reservations clerk looked up from the keyboard of the company's computer.

"Good morning, sir, how may I help you?" The voice was mechanical, without inflection.

Dotsero took her in with a practiced glance. Local girl, late teens or early twenties. Short hair cut in bangs which hung over vacant eyes. Face set in a bovine expression of contentedness as she chewed her gum in a slow methodical way.

"I need a car for a few days. Got stranded here when my companion was forced to return home earlier than planned."

"Size?"

"Subcompact would be fine."

"Gees. I'm sorry but I just rented out the only one."

"You know, I could wait if they are going to return that one within the next day or so."

"Just a minute."

She turned to her keyboard and tapped out a series of commands. "Sorry, that one is a one-way for drop off at Albuquerque International. I am expecting one to be dropped here in another three days."

"No problem, I'll take a midsize if you have one available."

Within minutes, Dotsero was on his way to Albuquerque. He estimated that he was about fifteen minutes behind John and started to push it. By the time, he reached the on-ramp for northbound I-25, he had him in sight.

****

By the time they reached the intersection of 152 and 35, Harkness guessed that Zack was headed back into the Gila Wilderness. When Zack turned north on 35 Harkness continued east in search of a phone. He found one at a Sinclair station just west of Kingston and called the motel.

"Feather Arrow Motel."

"Room 17, please."

The phone rang three times before the motel switchboard cut in.

"There is no answer, sir. Do you wish to leave a message?"

"Yes, this is Mr. Harkness. Please tell Mr. Dotsero that I have the permits for our backpacking trip and I will meet him at the Upper Black Canyon trailhead."

****

Zack caught sight of the grey Chevy Caprice with the coat hanger antenna in his rearview mirror as he turned north on 35. The Chevy continued east. Something was tugging at the back of his mind. Something about the Chevy. What was it? Then it hit him, he had seen that car. In fact, he had seen that car several times in the past few weeks. Damn, he was being followed.

Chapter Nineteen

Zack already gained the high ground on the opposite side of Diamond Creek by the time Harkness doubled back to pull into the upper trailhead parking area. He pulled into a parking slot next to Zack's Scout. As he maneuvered into the slot, he reflected on the fact that it didn't matter where he parked this time because neither Perry nor Johnson would live to see him, his car, or anything else.

He scribbled a brief map and note to Dotsero indicating the direction he was heading and after shoving it up into the springs under the front seat, he stepped out of the car.

A loud boom of thunder startled him and looking skyward he noticed the threatening cloud base hovering over the Black Mountains for the first time. "Shit," he thought. "Fucking weather." Wishing for a warm fire and a drink, he started north toward the Diamond Creek trail.

Zack watched the storm gather for the better part of the morning from his vantage point, overlooking his back trail. He purposely left signs marking his turnoff at 163 and Diamond Creek. If he was being followed, he wanted to find out who and why.

There was another loud crack of thunder close on the heels of a lightning flash. It looked like after several false starts the rainy season was finally here. He liked the rain, always had. He grew very fond of it in Nam, rain was good hunting weather. People let their guard down and were more interested in their comfort than their security. Yeah, he liked the rain just fine.

His patience was rewarded by the sounds of loose rock sliding somewhere on his back trail. In a few moments, Harkness came into view.

Zack sat in stunned silence. What in the hell was Harkness doing here? Was he alone? He had never seen Harkness without Dotsero. Did that mean that Dotsero was also here? What the hell was going on? By the time he snapped out of it, Harkness crossed the creek bottom and started up his side. Zack just started to stand when the flash flood roared around a bend twenty yards upstream and bore straight down. Harkness looked toward the sound and let out a thin high yelp of fear and despair. Cursing his fat body, he made a wild scrambling attempt to reach high ground. He managed to gain a tenuous handhold on the rocks at the top of the embankment but was unable to overcome the combined force of his bulk and the suction of the flood waters creeping above mid-thigh with a relentless force.

Throwing his head backward as he strained against certain death, he opened his eyes and found Zack looking down at him.

"Thank God! Quick, Johnson give me a hand. I don't think I can hold on much longer." The wheedling tone of his voice set Zack's teeth on edge.

"I want some answers first."

"Christ, I'll drown, get me out, then we'll talk."

"Answers!"

"OK, OK."

"Why are you following me? And no bull shit. I'd just as soon leave you to die after what you and your buddy Dotsero pulled on me."

"I don't know what you mean. I never liked you much, but I never tried to hurt you."

"Cut the shit. You're in a pretty poor position to try a con job."

Harkness looked up into the coldest eyes he had ever seen and crumpled completely. He sobbed out the whole story from the accidental sighting in the restaurant in Las Cruces, Dotsero's belief that Zack was there to kill them both for what happened in Nam, and his suspicion of another motive: gold.

He whimpered through his sad tale, finishing with the statement that he and Dotsero were the only ones who knew of Zack and Perry's presence and he left a map for Dotsero to follow back at trail head in his car, in case Perry didn't lead him back.

Looking down into the doughy white face with its fear-stricken eyes, Zack couldn't tell where tears of terror and self-pity stopped and rain began. He was suddenly very tired and the distinction no longer held any importance whatsoever. Leaning forward, he grasped both of Harkness's ice-cold hands and pried them from the rock, looked into his eyes and let go. The water closed over him, immediately cutting off the cry of despair and disbelief before it began.

Chapter Twenty

Dotsero followed Perry into the terminal and watched as he turned in the keys and contract at the rental desk. He then followed Perry and watched as he entered Desert Air Service. Perry exited the offices about thirty minutes later with a DAS employee in tow and walked out to the flight line where they did a quick walk around a converted Sikorsky S-58 helicopter. A few minutes later, Perry was walking across the tarmac toward the AmFac Hotel and Dotsero was searching for a phone.

Twenty minutes after receiving Harkness's phone message from the motel switchboard, Dotsero was back on the road headed for the Gila Wilderness. He figured he had two things working for him. It was already early evening and that, combined with the storms that chased them both north, should keep Perry on the ground until the next morning. He should be back in the Gila in plenty of time to greet Perry personally.

Chapter Twenty-One

Zack gained the mesa by early afternoon and immediately started to clear out the remaining rock and rubble blocking easy access to the cavern. As he worked, his thoughts turned to the recent turn of events. He had to admit that Harkness was the last person he expected to see in this lifetime. He had no regrets for his part in the death of Harkness and he admitted a thrill of excitement at the thought of confronting Dotsero. He decided long ago not to seek revenge for what happened but if someone brought it to him he would finish it.

He then did something that he hadn't done since the hospital in Nam. He opened up that part of himself where the rage against Dotsero was buried and used it to clear the remaining rock. It felt good. By late afternoon, a sufficient path was cleared and he attained a very cold spot in his soul. He celebrated that coldness as he drifted off to sleep that night. He would need it when he dealt with Dotsero.

****

John was at the airport early enough to coincide his lift-off with the sun rising over the Sandias. The morning dawned bright and clear, the air washed fresh by yesterday's storms. The controls felt good in his hands. Although he kept his license current, it had been a while since he had flown and then it had been over the lushness of southeast Asia. The windswept barrenness spreading below him, interspersed with sections of lush green irrigated fields, was quite a contrast. Swinging onto his heading for the Gila, he reached cruising altitude when his stomach growled. No sweat. He should arrive in plenty of time for breakfast.

******

Dotsero stood on the edge of Diamond Creek in the predawn light. The water still surged through the narrow cut with tremendous force but seemed to be down somewhat from the high-water marks on the opposite bank. He found Harkness's message the previous evening, spent the night in his car, and set out as soon as he could see. Since he hadn't run into Harkness, he figured that he must have been able to cross before the rain choke creek rose to the level it had.

He decided to head upstream and look for a place to cross. He then cut back on the opposite bank until he crossed Harkness's trail and they were able to join forces. He knew Harkness may have continued trailing Johnson but he was certain that he would never confront him alone. Harkness was waiting for him up ahead, he was sure of that.

******

Zack looked up from his breakfast fire with a feeling of unease. It was a matter of moments before he was able to identify the source of his discomfort. The first whup, whup, whup of the approaching copter broke the early morning stillness. Those damn things always could send him back to the Nam, even if for only a moment.

He smiled as he set out an extra plate, cup, knife, fork, and spoon. Then he added another packet of eggs and more water to the dehydrated mix he was stirring.

Chapter Twenty-Two

They settled down around the fire with tin plates full of scrambled eggs, potato pancakes, and a Dolly Madison donut apiece, compliments of John.

Zack swallowed another mouthful of eggs. "Have any trouble leasing the bird?"

"Not a bit. I told them I was working for a group of investors that wanted to look at land around here and other spots in southwestern New Mexico with a final destination of Mexico City. Then I'm to bring the chopper back to Albuquerque. We have it for five days. We just better pull this off because it took every bit of our cash reserves for insurance, permits, fuel, and security deposit. Now, how about you? You have any trouble?"

Zack poured his second cup of coffee, settled himself on the ground, and leaning back against a downed log told John of his encounter with Harkness.

"Jesus, oh Jesus Christ, you killed him?"

"Yes, I did."

"But why? You could have done something else. You didn't have to kill him. We could have walked away from this."

Zack waited patiently until John ran out of steam. John was like a lot of people who just couldn't seem to understand that sometimes you just don't have any choice, sometimes you just do what has to be done and leave it at that.

"I don't know if you can understand this or not. There was nothing else I could have done that would have made any sense. It has nothing at all to do with the gold. Those bastards planned to kill me years ago. Harkness admitted it, there was no reason to believe he had changed his mind. Their mistake was in not making sure. I don't make mistakes like that. Dotsero is also on his way here and when he gets here, I'll be waiting and he is going to die."

John opened his mouth but before he could speak Zack silenced him with an upraised hand. "Look, John, you weren't anywhere near here when Harkness bought it. His death will be chalked up to one more careless backpacker and even if it's not there is no way it could be traced to me and certainly not to you. There is nothing you can do or say that will stop me from killing Dotsero. I don't need or want your help and I wouldn't take it even if you offered. What I want you to do is help me load the chopper and then I want you to take your gear and clear out until tomorrow morning. We should have plenty of time to do that."

"How can you be so sure?"

"I know that Dotsero followed you to Albuquerque yesterday. The earliest he could have gotten back here was last night. I know Dotsero, he would never try that trail in the dark, and even if he did, he'd be stopped by the creek. The only logical place to cross during a flood like that is upstream and the closest place to do it is three hours away. He can't possibly be here before early evening."

John had sat quietly while Zack was talking. He looked at Zack with new understanding. He remained quiet for several minutes and then said, "I know that you're right. I don't like it, but I know you're right. I'll help."

"Thanks, but no thanks," Zack said, holding up a hand to ward off John's anticipated protest. "I appreciate the offer but you would only be in the way. You fly choppers, I kill people. Let's stick to what we've been trained to do. Now, let's get that gold on board."

Chapter Twenty-Three

Dotsero crept up to the lip of the mesa top slowly. It got decidedly rougher after he abandoned the trail some two hundred yards back. He was able to pick up the trail after a six-hour detour and followed it with total confidence until a sixth sense cautioned him to get off it. Something must have happened to Harkness. He should have made contact by now. Another black cloud blocking the sun momentarily caused him to glance skyward again. The buildup of thunderheads was mute testimony of more rain yet to come. How he loathed this country.

Slowly raising his head over the edge and parting some scrub brush in front of his face, he looked out onto the mesa top. The chopper stood silently on its skids on the far side of the mesa near the base of the cliff. A small camp consisting of a dome tent and backpacks stood off to the left of the gaping tunnel's mouth. There was no one in sight. At that moment, the sun broke out from behind the bank of clouds and a single ray struck the gold stacked on the floor of the chopper. Dotsero was mesmerized by the sight; he didn't know the details of how yet, but he had to have it. Pausing for a moment, he checked his service revolver and then started his approach to the camp using the mesa's sparse cover to his maximum advantage.

Zack sensed the presence of another human before he heard anything of consequence. He was laying in the shallow depression, covered with loose dirt, for about an hour. Although John argued against the wisdom of burying himself in the ground as foolhardy since if anything went wrong he wouldn't have any place to go or room to maneuver in, Zack held fast to his plan and in the end John agreed. He buried Zack and brushed out any sign that would give away his position just to the left of the tunnel's entrance. Any sign that he may have missed was obliterated by a light shower that broke immediately following John's departure.

Dotsero was about two-thirds of the way across the mesa's top and still no sign of anyone. Had he misjudged Harkness? Had he already been there and taken care of the situation? He stopped about 50 feet away from the camp and situated himself behind a large boulder, and settled down to wait.

Zack estimated that it had been about an hour between the time the movement on the mesa stopped and then started again.

Good old Dotsero; never did have the patience for this kind of work. It was another few minutes before he heard him poking around the tent and then the chopper. Zack paid close attention to monitoring his breathing as Dotsero passed within a few feet of his self-imposed grave. As soon as Dotsero passed, Zack began to raise his upper body with a soundless fluid movement. Dotsero's unprotected back was turned toward him and for just a moment, he considered shooting him where he stood. The necessity for an accidental death ruled out that option. Continuing his movement, he finished extracting himself and placing the muzzle of his pistol behind Dotsero's right ear said, "Been a long time, asshole."

Chapter Twenty-Four

"Loose the pistol and get your hands up." Dotsero did as he was told. Zack gave him a quick single-handed pat down for any concealed weapons and found none.

"Turn slowly and go over to the camp."

"What are you doing? Who the hell are you anyway?"

"Shut up and don't turn around until I tell you."

Zack didn't know whether it was the tone of voice, the gun, or a combination of both but Dotsero complied without resistance. They reached the tent, and stepping away from Dotsero, Zack said, "You can turn around now."

Dotsero turned slowly and then let his face show surprise.

"Johnson, Zackary Johnson, is that really you?" Dotsero was lowering his hands as he started toward Zack with a look of bewilderment and pleasure on his face.

"Hold it right there and cut the crap. I've already talked to Harkness." Zack's voice was like ice.

Dotsero's expression crumpled into defeat.

"Well, why don't you get him out here? We can all talk about it."

"He has said all he is ever going to say on that or any other subject. See that sleeping bag? Get into it now."

123

Dotsero picked up the bag Zack indicated. It was a widely used type of sleeping bag called a "mummy" because of its design, wide at the shoulders, tapering to a narrow foot with a two-way zipper, allowing access from either end. It was topped off with a hood and complete with drawstring. Once it was occupied, only the occupant's face was exposed to the elements. It served not only as a sleeping bag but in this case, also as a quasi-prison, preventing any sudden movements on the part of its occupant.

Zack made himself comfortable, stoking up the fire in anticipation of the chill of early evening.

He looked over at Dotsero. "Let's finish that conversation we were having back in Laos. Seems to me you were going to explain about you not being involved in the drug trade. Now, we can save some time. Harkness already admitted both of you were involved. What I want to know is why? You knew where those drugs were going, either to the States or for sale to our own guys over there. Why?"

Through the whole exchange, Zack's voice was devoid of any emotion and Dotsero's face gave away nothing.

"Money, and more money, plain and simple. I mean, what were you there for? Mom, God, and apple pie? You naive kids make me sick. Between you and your kind believing in a military strategy that was doomed from the start and the peace freaks in the States and over there working in the refugee camps, no one woke up to the fact that we weren't supposed to win that war. The way the politicians were working it, there was no way we could. So, why not make the best of a bad situation and make a few bucks on the side? And don't get righteous with me. I wasn't holding a gun on anyone to use that shit. Besides, when everything is breaking down isn't it the American way for everyone to take care of himself and fuck the other guy?"

Zack let the silence following Dotsero's explanations build for several minutes.

"You finished? I don't agree. Maybe I've mellowed enough to be able to look at your viewpoint and try to understand it but it doesn't really matter. What matters is that you left me to the jungle and the VC. You screwed up royally and you're going to die for it. The only thing I haven't quite figured out is how."

He glanced over Dotsero's shoulder at the silent chopper sitting some ten yards away. Dotsero followed his gaze and a realization slowly dawned. A fine sheen of sweat formed on his forehead and a convulsive shudder shook his body.

"You remember, don't you? Yeah, you remember. You remember how much you used to enjoy the interrogations?

Remember how we would load them into the choppers and go up about three hundred feet and hover? Remember grabbing the ones we suspected had the least information and hauling them over to the doorway and shoving their heads out and making them look down? Remember how they'd say they didn't know when we questioned them and how some of them would fill the chopper with the stench of empty bowels and bladders and then we would throw them out and watch them run to the ground? You know something? I've always wondered why they almost always ran. Remember, betting on where their bodies would hit? And then after the others told us everything they knew, we'd throw them out too? Do you remember it? I do. I will for the rest of my life. Yeah, they were the enemy, but they were human beings too. Well, I was just wondering, will you scream and cry? Will you run to the ground? Will you dump your bladder and bowels?"

Dotsero didn't say a word; the sweat on his forehead shone in the firelight, he didn't demonstrated any reaction at all. He just sat there with a sullen expression. Several minutes of silence were finally broken.

"You know what your trouble is? You talk too much. Just do it or let me go."

Dotsero seemed to have a moment of inspiration. "You're not going to do it, are you? I'm white. They were only a bunch of gooks. Now, let me out of here."

Without a word, Zack got up and walked to the edge of the firelight. Stooping, he picked up a burlap sack bound at the open end by a drawstring that until this moment escaped Dotsero's notice. The sack rolled with a motion very much like thick oatmeal coming to a slow boil. As he approached the sleeping bag, a dry rattle issued from the burlap sack. Dotsero began to buck and thrash about wildly.

"I'd hold still if I were you. You don't want to agitate my friend here. It's not healthy."

And with that, Zack opened the sleeping bag from the bottom and with one fluid motion stuffed the open end of the sack into the end of the sleeping bag, pulled the drawstring, dumped the rattler in and closed the zipper.

Dotsero froze when the snake dropped into the bag. By craning his neck, he watched with a morbid curiosity as it moved slowly up between his legs and finally settled in a coil against the heat of his crotch. The minutes ticked by slowly, his scrotum shriveled. By this time, the sweat was pouring freely down his face.

"Kill it, kill it and I'll give you whatever you want!" His voice was a thin raspy whisper.

"You don't get it, do you? After he strikes, I'll let you out. Who knows, if he hits you low and you move easily you might make it."

At that moment, the rattler struck Dotsero in the inner thigh. Measuring the distance later, Zack determined Dotsero made almost one hundred yards before he died.

Chapter Twenty-Five

Zack stretched and rolled over on the blanket. It had been two weeks since John left with the gold.

He received confirmation from Switzerland this morning. His share, less handling fees, came out at ten million plus. He contemplated the handling fees again. Two million seemed like quite a lot but when it was measured against the problems of moving that much gold, it was rather reasonable. John's Bangkok contacts did a good job all the way from bribing the proper officials at the airport in Mexico City to moving the gold back to Bangkok. John was back in Thailand working with Patsy.

The authorities found the bodies of Dotsero and Harkness. The coroner's inquest ruled accidental death after determining that Harkness must have drowned going for help after Dotsero was bitten.

Yeah, things had worked out just fine.

He lay there with his arm across his eyes to block the afternoon sun's rays. He knew he would have to figure out what he was going to do next, that it was important to have a direction. But for now, he would settle for another piece of Pam's fried chicken and some more potato salad. Moving slowly so as not to disturb the figure asleep beside him, he sat up and reached for the picnic basket.

Chapter Twenty-Six

The setting sun glinted off the snow-covered crest of the mountain range that marked the western edge of their property. He lowered his gaze to watch as the shadows spread across the meadow before plunging the scene into twilight. Propping his dusty boots on the front porch railing of the spacious log home, he took a sip from the one whiskey a day that he allowed himself and settled into the rump-sprung easy chair. He heard the screen door behind him open and bang shut followed by a familiar and comfortable hand on his shoulder.

"Penny for your thoughts," said Pam.

"Look at that sunset," Zach replied.

Pam pulled a sister-chair towards the railing and said, "I never tire of this time of day."

"Neither do I. I was thinking of how grateful I am to have you," and with an all-encompassing wave of his hand, "for us to have all of this," indicating the roughly 10,000 acres they owned.

They had purchased the property some time ago after Zack decided to return to his family roots of cattle ranching. They found the perfect site. The ranch consisted of expansive grasslands watered by springs and a year-round river. This was interspersed with stands of pine and fir. The grazing could not have been better with more than ample food for their large herd of cattle.

The wildlife was bear, elk, mule deer, mountain lion, and turkey. Over the years, they turned down multiple requests to allow hunting. After achieving a different perspective, being shot at instead of shooting at, Zack had not touched a firearm since his return from Nam. He was more interested in preserving life than ending it.

Relishing in the comfortable companionship of shared silence he had to admit, life was good.

About the Author

This is Scott Miller's first novel. He lives in the Pacific Northwest where he is currently at work on his second novel.